The universe of variant time-tracks controlled by the civilization of Vroom was one of variety and mystery. There were worlds where mankind had been destroyed in atomic war, worlds where Aztecs still ruled North America or the Vikings had established ascendancy . . . even worlds where mankind had never existed! And the men who patrolled these alternate worlds were strong and resourceful, backing their technology with the force of telepathic mind-control.

Wardsman Blake Walker had not been born of Vroom, and he had none of their mind-powers—but on him rested the fate of the entire universe of time-tracks!

QUEST
CROSSTIME

QUEST CROSSTIME

ANDRE
NORTON

SF
ace books

A Division of Charter Communications Inc.
A GROSSET & DUNLAP COMPANY
51 Madison Avenue
New York, New York 10010

QUEST CROSSTIME

DEDICATION

For Richard Benyo,

who first visualized the "sterile" world.

This Printing: JANUARY 1981
Published Simultaneously in Canada
Printed in U.S.A.

I

THE LAND REPELLED. Not because of any raw breakage, for the rocky waste was contoured by wind and storm, the wind and water of passing centuries. But those gray, red-brown, lime-white strata were only that; bare stone. And their colors were muted, somber. Even the sea waves, washing with constant booming force at the foot of the cliff, were a steely shade today under the massing clouds of another storm. It was a world completely alienated from the present struggle centered in a cluster of green hemispheres in the river valley below; a world which had had no dealing with humankind, nor with animals, nor birds, nor reptiles, nor even the simplest forms of celled life such as might float in the water. For this was a world in which no spore of life had ever dwelt— sterile rock—until man, with his restless drive for change, had chosen to trouble its austerity.

The storm now gathering would be a bad one. Marfy Rogan looked up at the piling clouds, assessed the growing twilight they brought. She was a fool to linger here. Still . . .

She did not get to her feet. Instead, she leaned forward in the niche she had found, rested her forehead on the crook of her arm, pressing her shoulder against the harsh surface of the supporting rock. Her body was tense with the effort she put into her searching probe. In her, what had begun as a momentary uneasiness had long since grown into a fire of fear.

"Marva!" Her lips moved soundlessly as she sent that cry, by another method than speech, out into the vast wilderness of this lifeless successor world. The sea's clamor might even have drowned out a shout, but it could not deter the call she sent mind to mind. Only—that receptive other mind was not there!

And that silence meant a contradiction which was the root of her fear. For among the other equipment fastened to the belt of her work suit was a small instrument ticking serenely away, reporting that all was well, that Marva, to whose body it was—or had been—tuned, was going about her business in a normal way. *Had* been tuned . . .

Any change in that personality setting would indicate willful interference. What would be the cause of such a starkly mad act? Naturally, those on the field trip would take cover when they saw the storm warnings and not try to return to Headquarters. But distance was no barrier to the tie between the twin sisters, no reasonable distance. And the 'copter was neither supplied nor prepared to make any long trek over the unending desert of rock.

Marva's personnel disk reported all well with her, but Marfy's mind and inner sense denied that vehemently. And of the two, she depended first upon her own senses. Yet the disk testified against her.

Had there been anyone down in the camp other than Isin Kutur, Marfy would have been spilling out her worries an hour ago. But he made it so plain that he resented their arrival, that he would joyfully and speedily seize any means that would allow him to bundle them back into the level shuttle and be rid of them, that she had not gone down. And in that she had been a coward. Because if what she was beginning to suspect was true . . .

Marfy lifted her head. Her fine, fair hair was netted against the wind's violence, her face now bare of all the conventional cheek- and forehead-stenciling fashionable in her set. She closed her eyes, the better to "see" with that other sense roving in frantic search. Delicate features, a skin which was ivory pale, with only closely pressed lips providing color, her face had the elegance of line that came from centuries of breeding, tending, and cherishing. So that in her present rocky setting she was as fantastically placed as a flower growing from the stone.

"Marva!" Her voiceless summons was a scream. But there was no answer.

The questing fingers of the wind pulled at her. Marfy opened her eyes just as the first spattering drops of rain hit the rocks with increasing force. She could not descend the cliff path to camp now, she dare not set her strength against the force of that rising gale, the drowning downpour. In her desire to get away from observation in the camp, she had both chosen worse and better than she had been aware of at the time: worse, in that she must be hidden from sight below and temporarily lost as far as they were concerned; better, in that by squirming farther back into the niche, she had shelter from the worst of the storm.

So, hidden in the depths of that crevice, she could no longer see the rush of wind-lashed sea or anything else, beyond a slice of gray sky now and then traced with the brilliance of unleashed lightning. Judging by her past experience of these storms, she had perhaps an hour or so to remain here.

"Marva!" She loosed a last appeal, waited with dulled and dying hope.

Marva, contrary to all "rightness," was beyond contacting. Yet the disk said she was present, not too far away, and all was well with her. Thus—the disk lied. And yet that, by everything Marfy had been told or taught, was impossible!

When they had come crosstime to this Project, they had been given the most careful briefing, indoctrinated with the need for protection devices. And Marva—as adventurous, as impatient of control as she sometimes was—was not ever really reckless. Nor would her sister have begun a new adventure without Marfy; they had always acted together in any important thing.

Also, there was no reason in the world—this world or any other of the myriad ones open to their people—why their activities would be interfered with to the extent of making a personnel disk lie. Why, as much as Kutur resented them, it was to his own advantage to see they had Hundred treatment. They were Erc Rogan's daughters, traveling with his official permission on a carefully charted crosstime quest for knowledge.

Unless—Marfy's head jerked as a sudden thought startled her. Unless the Limiters . . . She licked raindrops from her lips. Marva oftentimes accused her of having a suspicious mind. As twin sisters they might be one in most things, but there were basic differences of emotion, spirit, intellect;

they were individuals, not just two halves of a split whole. The Limiters was the party behind the growing demand that crosstime travel be placed under strict control. Supervised and controlled, of course, by Saur To'Kekrops' proposed committee—which was the same as saying To'Kekrops and his liege men alone. If there was an incident which could be used for public report, proving the dangerous quality of crosstime exploration, the need for rigid supervision; an accident to some member of the Hundred or to the family of such a member—Marfy sucked in her breath, went rigid. But To'Kekrops would not *dare!* And how could he interfere?

There was no possible entrance into this successor world except right down there in the midst of camp. And no possible travel vehicle except the official shuttles. Also, the Project personnel would and did have no sympathy with the Limiters. Their experiments here would be among the first to be canceled under such a regimen.

Marva . . .

The fury of the storm was a battle over and around Marfy's small crack of safety. She had witnessed by proxy such explosions of nature pictured on the record tapes in the library of crosstime Headquarters. It had been four centuries—no, five now—since her people had unlocked the gates of Vroom's time and had gone, not backward nor forward, but across the fabric of counted years to visit other successor worlds whose history followed tracks varying further and further from that of Vroom. For, from decisions made in history, sometimes even from the death of a single man, separated worlds split, divided, and re-divided, to make a littering web of time roads, some so divergent that those who used them were no longer wholly human as she and her kind defined human.

And this was one of the oddest of those alternate worlds, one in which the first cells of life had never come into being at all: water, stone, soil, wind, rain, sun. But nothing living or growing. Then the Project had moved in to sow life, or attempt to do so, under controlled conditions. And the experiment was the ride of one of the great scientific groups electing twenty of the ruling Hundred. No, Project personnel would do nothing to jeopardize what they were attempting to accomplish here.

Marva had been restless during the past few days. She liked people. The thrill of crosstime travel was allied in her with a chance to study other levels which were not barren deserts. The sisters had made two such trips, having sworn to obey orders, and both times Marva had been disappointed at the narrow path they had been constrained to walk. Here they had been afforded more freedom, simply because there were no other-world natives to whom they could inadvertently reveal themselves.

So—But there was no use in speculating, although Marfy's imagination continued to supply her with a series of explanations drawn from the few facts she knew, each perhaps a little more exotic than the one preceding it. Only one decision for her, once the storm was over: she was going straight to Kutur. Then she was going to demand what she had been so careful not to request since they had arrived and had learned that

Kutur's compliance with Erc Rogan's request for their visit had been a very unwilling one: she was going to demand a message right, and report directly to—to whom?

Erc Rogan was level-hopping, inspecting successor depots, making sure the Limiters had no laxness of regulation, no possible excuse to enter a "contrary" at the next conference. She might catch him in any of half a hundred stations. But also she would have to leave calls at each, and she dared not tie up the message lines unless it was a matter of dire importance. The very leaving of those calls would cause comment and stir across the whole crosstime system.

Then, to whom? Com—Com Varlt perhaps? She had known Com since he had been an Aptwardsman just out of training, when she and Marva had been taken, at the age of six, to see the animals on the Forest Level. Com Varlt's family holdings marched with Rogan's; they had interfamilied twice in the not too-distant past. And Varlt was on home duty this month. Yes, a message to Varlt, though they would wonder about that, too. Unless Marva . . . Marfy shook her head in answer to her own thoughts, willing away that hot, tight feeling inside that threatened to take over her emotions whenever she thought of her sister and the unanswered mind call. She would wait out the storm up here; the time would give her a chance to think out just the right message for Varlt. Then, once the worst of the wind and rain was over, she would go back to camp, face up to Kutur, and claim her right of communication.

It was a small shuttle but compact. Not with all

the latest fixtures, of course, but well fitted for such a routine run. Blake Walker glanced about the small cabin. Two cushioned and shielded seats were in place before the control board; behind them, the lockers of emergency supplies, recording equipment, tools. It was as safe a method of crosstime travel as the experts—and they were expert—had been able to devise to date. A satisfactory standing at his passout from instruction into the corps allowed him to make this routine run alone.

In a package wedged behind his seat was the ostensible reason for his trip: special scientific equipment to be delivered to a project attempting to seed life on a sterile world. His other mission had been delivered orally by Master Wardsman Com Varlt: to check on the Rogan twins.

Not too long ago, before the Limiters had become so vocal—and why had their reactionary party become suddenly so important, backed by a huge increase in membership—crosstime travel had provided holidaying for responsible parties, field trips for students, and the usual business of trades. But there had been a cutback in permits when the Limiters began fulminating opposition. Now word had come down the line with emphasis: no more pleasure travel save to "empty" forest worlds, nothing to cause incidents. And that had not been too smart a move, for it played into To'Kekrops' hands in the other direction. He now demanded why, if crosstiming was so safe, did they refuse permits? Rogan had fought the cutback in outgo permissions, had declared it the wrong answer to To'Kekrops' insinuations, and, to prove that, had pointedly defied the order, sending his daughters on a student permission to the Project. He had had to answer one Question for that, but he had stuck to his beliefs, and was using his position to reinstate the normal traffic.

Blake wriggled against the protecting cushions of his seat. He had worked out his own travel code and had it checked. Now he proceeded to put the pattern into action on the board. Even veteran master wardsmen were never hasty about coding, and the requirement of making three checks before the pattern was loosed did not make any shuttle pilot impatient. A fraction of an inch either way might not only land him on the wrong level, but might also mean death because the shuttle might well materialize in a position of space already firmly occupied by some massive solid object.

So Blake took his time, made three checks before playing out the pattern on the hand keys. There was a whir, the sickening lurch to break free from stable time on Vroom's level and go voyaging across the worlds of alternate destinies.

Sealed in the cabin, Blake caught no glimpse of those worlds, not even as shadows flowing about him, although the first time he had so traveled, on the secret shuttle of a level-hopping criminal, he had seen them gather, break, reform, change beyond the bare rim of the platform on which he had huddled. He himself had come out of one of those other worlds, caught up, through no will of his own but because of a psi gift, in the affairs of Com Varlt's team of man hunters. They had played out a wild game then, and in the end the team had had no choice but to take Blake on to Vroom, since his defensive inborn mind-block made false memory grafting impossible.

A stranger in his own world, where he had been found as a baby in an alley and fostered by those who had died before he was fully grown, Blake accepted Vroom's friendship and the offer of a career as wardsman. And he knew that, though it had never been fully proved, Com Varlt believed that he, Blake, came from yet another level, one close to Vroom and on the verge of discovering crosstiming itself when a chain atomic reaction had destroyed it utterly. Was he the only survivor of that world? Had he been the child of some experimenter there who had seen a slim chance of survival for his son by putting him through a yet untested "door"? Perhaps. But his possible parentage was no longer of any consequence to Blake. He was well content with what Vroom had to offer, and secretly more than satisfied with the chance to make this solo run.

Once set up and in progress, the code pattern acted independently of the shuttle's pilot. He had a little more than an hour, if time was to be reckoned under such circumstances. But speculation on that point did not bother Blake.

No wardsman wore uniform save for ceremonial occasions at Vroom. You might possess the short maroon jacket, the tight-fitting breeches, metal-latched boots for all your days of service in the corps and perhaps appear only three or four times with those articles of dress on your back and body. Blake's lean, six-foot frame was clothed now in the same drab coveralls as he would find the Project men wearing when the shuttle reached his destination. Above this monotone of color, his brown skin, a smooth brown which was its natural pigment rather than any tan, seemed even darker. Sharp in contrast, in the bright interior light of the shuttle cabin, was his hair, a dark red. He wore the equipment belt of an explorer, its various gadgets for defense or survival use. And around his neck the corps identification tag slipped, cool against his flesh, as he moved.

He had made three runs since he passed out of instruction, all as the least important member of temporary crews on routine missions. And he had yet to serve as a "passer" or part of a contact crew more or less permanently in residence on any foreign level. Sometimes such a stint called for plastic surgery and study techniques that altered the team beyond the point of any return, so its members had to pass through a reversal of procedure when their tour of duty was finished. But one had to be at least two steps higher in rank and well tested before one could qualify for that. Also, one had to be really "talented." All the fabled psi gifts of his native level were known to the wardsmen some of whom possessed two or even more. Levitation, telepathy, telekinesis, precognition— Blake had seen them all in action and also in testing. But compared with most of his fellow corpsmen in service or training, he had but meager natural equipment.

His two "talents," if so they might be termed, were precognition of danger, which he had experienced all his life—in the past to his uneasy concern—and another which he had not known he possessed until he had met the wardsmen during their hunt for the escaped criminal. But in this second talent Blake was not only the equal of his new companions—he was their superior. For without willing it or training, he had developed a mind block to the degree that no one he had yet met—and in the course of training he had been confronted with the best his commanding officers could throw at him—might influence his thinking or read his thoughts. In a telepathic society he possessed a natural defense better than any perfected by mechanical means.

Blake had tried to develop other talents, hoping that esper powers might be latent. But his most rigorous struggles had ended in failure. It was the lack of these talents that might keep him grounded when it came to regular crosstime missions. Like the ache of a long-suffered wound, suppressed but ever there, that thought lay at the back of Blake's mind.

However, there would be no call for esper talents at the Project. He would deliver this package, observe the situation as far as the Rogan girls were concerned, and be on his way back in a matter of hours. A dull task all around. Next tour ought to be Forest Level and that was better. A world without men, where animals were free and without fear, the Forest Level was a favorite with children and family groups for camping. Three wardsmen accompanied each so-arranged tour and all protective "waves" were always on. So far no protest from the Limiters for a close-down there had been voiced. Forest World was too popular. To'Kekrops' party would risk a vast amount of adverse reaction if they tried making that level out of bounds.

Light flashed on his board. Blake's hand hovered over the key as he counted up to ten and then down again, giving the double amount of time to assure himself complete arrival. Then he flicked the hatch release. The shuttle ceased to quiver, a portion of the wall moved, and Blake looked out into the faintly bluish light of the level terminal.

Blake blinked as he recognized the man facing him—Tursha Scylias, second-in-command of the whole Project. Whatever he transported must be more important than he had been informed. He pulled the package out of its tight fittings, lifting it with the care he supposed it deserved.

But Scylias accepted the burden almost absently, continuing to eye Blake.

"You are new." Not a question but a flat statement.

"On this run, yes," Blake answered, refusing to admit to this man how new he was. Because there was a metallic taste in his mouth, a prickle of roughening skin between his shoulders. Trouble! Here—or very close! He was alerted by his talent, and instantly, in only half-conscious effort, his mind shield went up. This much he had learned under tuition, to maintain before that shield a defense of camouflage surface thought. And, in times of stress, a second and deeper layer would deceive all but the expert into thinking he was not shielded at all.

Now he stepped from the hatch, his boots stamping on the undisguised rock that formed the floor of the camp structure, wishing he had some telepathic power to pick up from Scylias a hint of what the trouble was.

"Reports." The assistant Project leader whipped out two rolls of tape in a carrying case. He made no move to step out of Blake's way; it was as if he had to keep a tight hold on himself to avoid herding the wardsman straight back into the machine. Then perhaps he himself recognized that suspicious attitude, for he did not demur when Blake set the record case within the hatch and turned once more to his greeter.

"Everything satisfactory?" Blake fell back on the official report terms.

"Entirely so," Scylias replied and then added harshly, "You will eat with us? It is the mid hour."

"Good enough. Thank you. I'll just check the message station . . ."

Scylias moved as if to block Blake's movement toward the outward entrance of the terminal and to guide it instead to the tunnel connecting that room with other parts of the camp.

"Storming out." His tone was flat. "You cannot reach the rods until that is over."

Trouble . . . trouble . . . The pulse was beating heavily behind Blake's eyes now. Not the storm, no, but perhaps the rods . . . But why? No sane project leader or member would allow any trouble with the rods! To be cut off with no chance of getting a message through. They could not want that. But what was wrong with Scylias? The man was definitely on edge. And there was danger here—bad—from the way Blake felt now.

II

PERHAPS BECAUSE there was no vegetation to act as wind breaks, the storm seemed to have more force than on a normal world. Blake stared out of a viewport at the rush of wind-driven rain striking against the camp shelters. They were located in a valley, the only break between cliff walls for a long stretch of territory. Blake need only turn his head to see the map of the Project set out on the curving wall. The valley was cut by an unusually slow-flowing river which formed a small delta of silt at its sea mouth. And the sea itself was provided with a breakwater of curving reef, turning the river-mouth coast into a partly sheltered bay.

Along the nearer bank of the river were the growth tanks, carefully sown and now housing the algae and other primitive life imported from the Vroom laboratories. This was only the beginning of the Project, but Blake knew that a fantastic amount of labor and capital had already gone into it.

Crosstime travel was largely trade, discreet trade, and the real foundation of all Vroom's economy. Trade from one successor world to another, natural resources from underdeveloped and primitive levels, luxuries from more sophisticated civilizations—never enough taken to cause native comment or investigation. And if now useless levels such as this could be harvested, then Vroom, apart from the knowledge gained in experimentation, would be that much richer and more securely buttressed against the future.

Outside the viewport the rain was forming so thick a curtain that Blake could not see the neighboring shelter as more than a vague outline. He turned to the map with some interest, and then passed along to view the series of taped scenes mounted in a panorama of color: always only rock, or sea, or rivers and lakes in stone settings. The color of that rock varied, sometimes brighter and more eye-catching, but never bearing any hint of green life. And, as Blake studied those pictures, the uneasiness that had ridden him since he had disembarked from the shuttle grew sharper. Though he had ostensibly been viewing the outer world since he had been shown into this lounge by Scylias, he had been listening with all the effort he could muster for any sound.

So far Blake had seen none of the other personnel. He was trying to recall all he knew of the fellowship of the Project. Isin Kutur headed it. The man had a reputation for being a driver, single-minded, one who bulled through shaky causes but shed friends, or rather acquaintances, along the way. His standing with the Hundred was high. Twice he had pulled out of difficulty, or salvaged, expensive projects about to be written off as failures. Blake had seen him on a televised cast, a stolid, thick-shouldered man, with a shock of prematurely white hair, who had given impatient, monosyllabic answers to the interview questions.

Isin Kutur, Scylias—Blake searched his memory and found that was the extent of his acquaintance with the Project personnel. Except, of course, the Rogan twins, and them he knew only through Varlt's briefing. Daughters of a four-

generation Hundred family. Blake had studied
the picture of them Varlt had shown him, and in
his mind he could not match the stark utility of
this background with the girls who had appeared
there.

"Wardsman?" A woman stood in the doorway.
But not one of the Rogan girls. She was at least two
decades older, and her rather sharp-featured face
bore the crease of a permanent frown between
thick brows. "If you will come, we are about to
eat." Her speech was stilted; she was clearly not at
ease.

Blake followed her into a larger division of the
structure from which came the smell of food,
largely synthetics of the ration type. But those
gathering about the table were apparently welcoming the Spartan fare with gusto. Kutur was
seated with one elbow cushioned on a note board.
From time to time he scribbled quickly on that
archaic writing aid; otherwise he paid no attention to his surroundings.

There were five other staff members present:
the woman who had ushered Blake into the room;
Scylias, three more, one of them also a woman.
But of the Rogan girls there was no sign. And
since none of his tablemates seemed disposed to
talk, the wardsman hesitated to break the silence.
Kutur had not even looked up from his scribble
block. Blake sipped at the container of hot drink
and waited.

Trouble rang his inner alarm. But that was the
difficulty with his talent, he could not define the
danger or its source. That it was imminent he was
sure. And it was all he could do to curb his unease
and continue to sit at the table, nibble his unap-

petizing rations, and wait for enlightenment.

Kutur shoved the pad aside, raised his head and looked about. His attention flickered down one side of the table and up the other. When his glance reached Blake, he gave a sharp nod which might have been intended as a curt greeting or merely recognition of the younger man's place in the general scheme of things.

"Where is the girl?" It was not the voice one expected from that bull chest and thick throat. In place of a growl or a husky rumble, the words were delivered as a cultivated, almost melodious query. Blake had heard actors and orators with less natural ability to shape speech into rhythm.

"Marfy?" The woman who had been Blake's guide shot a glance to her left as if she expected to see someone there. The crease between her brows sharpened, her mouth twisted. She dropped the wafer she had been holding to her lips and swiftly detached a small disk from her belt, bringing it to her ear as she replied to Kutur. "She went up the cliff just before the storm, Head. But the signal is in order. The recall, we all heard the warning recall. She must have heard it too!"

Kutur surveyed them again, beginning with Scylias and following along the line. He even favored Blake with his searching stare.

"Evidently she did not hear it, or else she chose to disregard it. There is no place here for such foolishness. I have said it. I now repeat it many times, and loud enough for all fools to take it through their ear holes into their brains: there is no place in crosstime for foolishness! We have no time to hunt lost ones." Deliberately his thick fingers went to his own belt and he unhooked a twin to the coin-shaped object the woman still held. With one fingernail he gave it a vigorous tapping, then held it to his ear.

"She is in no danger," he stated. "Perhaps a wet skin and some discomfort will make her think next time. We cannot watch after children who will not obey the simplest and most obvious rules. So will you state this afternoon, Tursha, to the authorities. I shall have no further troubling from such visitors, no matter how many official cards they carry!"

One of the Rogans, Blake deduced, was out in the storm. But apparently the staff had some check on her which reassured Kutur, even if that did not testify to her exact whereabouts. But what of her sister? No one had mentioned the other girl at all.

They sat at a long table; there was plenty of unoccupied space around it. Blake tried to estimate who, beyond the two girls, might be missing. Dared he ask questions?

Chance seemed to be aiding him for Kutur spoke again. "The 'copter sheltered safely, I trust. No more foolishness to be reported?"

Scylias nodded. "Yes, they grounded at the first cloud massing. Garglos said they were running under a ledge big enough for full cover."

Kutur grunted. "For any trace of intelligence in one's subordinates one must offer thanks, exceedingly great thanks—or so it seems to me at present. You, wardsman, have you been given any orders for me? Any more limits to be set on what we may or may not do lest we, in some fashion, influence this stretch of rock into future ill behavior?"

From some men that might have been an attempt at humor, but to Blake it sounded like ponderous sarcasm. "Routine inspection of the rods, Head," he replied tersely.

Kutur nodded. "Very well. Do your duty, wardsman. But see me before you go. I will have a message, a personal message to be delivered to Hundredman Rogan. I will not"—he drove his pen spear-fashion into the surface of the scribble block—"I will not be bothered by school girls. This I am deciding now and for all time!"

Again he stared at each of the company in turn as if expecting someone to refuse what was clearly an ultimatum. But no one demurred.

A clearing of a throat brought all their attention to one of the men who had accompanied Scylias. "Storm is slacking off."

For a moment Blake wondered how the other could be sure of that in this windowless chamber. Then he was aware that the steady beat of rain, which had been a low drumming during all his time in Project Headquarters, was lessening. Kutur was already on his feet, ready for action.

"Ulad, Kyogle, down to the flats with me! We shall be most favored by fortune if the water has not ruined half twenty days' work."

"But Marfy?" the woman leaned forward to ask.

Kutur glared. His head swung around as if counting his followers. Then his finger stabbed at Blake.

"You! Your duty is to keep an eye on travelers, is it not? Then get out there and find this fool of a girl and bring her back, even if you have to drag her all the way!" He reached the door in a couple of strides and left Blake with the woman. In a way he was right, the wardsmen were primarily a protection force for Vroom's people in the network of alternate worlds. But where would he start here? The danger he sensed waiting around some shadowy corner, was it concerned with Marfy Rogan?

"She—she *has* been most foolish, you know," the woman said. "These storms are very severe, and we always sound a recall before they break. Every one of us carries one of these tuned to our personality." She indicated the disk at her belt. "If we are in trouble, it broadcasts a call for help to be picked up by every other disk. This is the best protection we have found in case of accident. Marfy is not in any danger. And there is a locater tuned to these which will guide you. Wait, I will get it for you from Head Kutur's office."

She trotted off and Blake fell in behind her. Then she darted into a door which she closed firmly in his face, to return a few moments later with a slightly larger disk equipped with a swinging, nervous needle.

"I have set it. I do not believe Head Kutur will mind my taking the liberty. He would have ordered it to be given to you had he had the time. But this rain . . . And if the river rises again, it may, as he said, wipe out much of our labor. We have had three of these rains in one week, and never before so many so close together. The problem of the excess water is becoming acute. Marfy has chosen the worst possible time to irritate Head Kutur when his mind must hold and solve so many problems! See, the needle is already swinging. Follow that and you will find her. Oh, take these also." She jerked open another door and pulled out two stormcoats complete with hoods.

Bundling both of these into Blake's hold, she thrust her long arms into the sleeves of a third, hurrying away from him as she adjusted the hood. So protected against the elements, with the extra coat under his arm and the homing device in his hand, Blake followed in her wake.

The terrific force of the storm might have slackened a little, but the rain still poured, hitting the rocks and then cascading in runnels down any inclined surface. The eye place in Blake's hood gave him a curtailed field of vision, and the needle on the dial swung away from the cluster of shelters by the river, pointing to the rocky cliff at his right.

Mud was glue to catch his boots, and Blake made the cliffward march with grim determination, finding few kindly thoughts for the object of his search. If this was a sample of the Rogan girls' behavior in the field, he did not wonder at Kutur's impatience. Only—his inner alert was still warning him.

The clouds parted to the west and thin sunshine made a pallid struggle against the gloom. Blake threw back the hood of his coat. The stark nature of the country was depressing in spite of the now clearing sky and the sun. One did not miss vegetation until there was a complete lack of it. One small struggling plant would have provided a very welcome break in this bleak landscape. If the Project succeeded in its experiments, there would be more than one plant in the river valley, but such a triumph of man over reluctant nature was still far in the future.

There were shouts in the valley, the purr of

motors. Blake glanced back. Machinery was moving out from under cover, heading for the swollen river and the walled pens, the barriers of which were now nearly hidden under the flooding waters. It would certainly appear that Kutur and his people had hard work before them.

Ahead of Blake was a path of sorts, more nearly a ladder where it climbed the heights. But before his boots were fairly set on that way there was movement above. Blake saw a slight figure in drab field dress, dark patches molding the fabric to upper arms and shoulders, hurrying along a ledge at what seemed to Blake a reckless pace. The girl was coming in his direction.

"Hoy!" The call was thin, distorted by faint echoes. An arm waved vigorously, signaling him to stay where he was.

She was surefooted, graceful, and competent as she descended that wet and perhaps treacherous ladder path. While she was still some distance away, he saw her stare at him, her eyes widen. Then she took the last drop with the ease of one following a known path.

Such was the difference between this wet and windblown figure and Varlt's picture that Blake might not have recognized her save under these circumstances. Her hair was braided and netted close to her head; she had none of the elaborate and exotic patterns stenciled on cheek and forehead after the latest fashion of Vroom. In spite of that, she looked older than he expected.

"You—you are not from the Project!" She had halted, her left arm flung out about a stone outcrop to break her last descent. Now she eyed him with something approaching suspicion.

"Walker, Ap-W 7105," he answered formally.

"Walker," she repeated as if the foreign-sounding name was in itself a matter for suspicion. "Walker!" That was recognition he had not expected. "Blake Walker! By the teeth of Pharses! Did Com Varlt send you? But how could he have known— Father! Something has happened to Father!" She left her rock anchor, skidded forward across a mud patch to catch at his arm with force enough nearly to send him off balance in turn.

"No, I'm making a routine run," Blake answered. "They found you missing from the camp, asked me to find you. Here, it looks as if there's another shower on the way. You had better get into this." He shook out the spare coat, swung it around her already soaked shoulders.

However, it was clear his reassurance had not relieved her concern. Through the hand still clutching his arm, Blake could feel her tension.

"What is it?" he asked in turn. She seemed to be unharmed, but he knew that Marfy Rogan was in more trouble than merely being caught in a storm.

"Marva! She went on a field trip in the 'copter this morning. And she is missing!"

Blake recalled the conversation at the table. "There was a message. The 'copter took shelter before the storm, perfectly safe—" Blake began, but the girl was determinedly shaking her head.

"She is not safe. Or at least she is not here."

"But these things"—Blake touched the disk on her belt—"would you not know about—"

Marfy tore the device from its hook, held it to his ear. "Listen!" She spoke with a fierce demand for immediate obedience. "Tell me, what do you hear?"

A throbbing beat, as steady as his own heart.

"Steady beating," he replied with the exact truth.

"Yes. And that is supposed to mean that there is nothing wrong, that Marva's out there some-where"—she made a sweeping gesture—"sit-ting under a rock, maybe eating rations with Nagen Garglos, waiting for the storm to clear so they can be back in time for evening meal. Only that is not the truth, not even a shadow of the truth!"

This was it, or part of it, his talent told him; this is what that inner alarm meant. And, so knowing, Blake was more than willing to listen. But what did she have to offer in the way of concrete fact?

"How do you know?"

Marfy Rogan frowned at him; there was some-thing of Kutur's unshaken self-confidence and arrogance in that expression. "Because we are twins, and we can mindspeak. We always have. I was down in camp this morning, in half-touch with Marva. Then—nothing!" She snapped her fingers. "Just like that—nothing at all! It has never happened before and—well—I thought for a while that I might be under a shield. Kutur has a lot of experimental installations, other projects send him things to try out in the atmosphere of this level. So when I was cut off I got out, away from camp, up here"—she waved now to the cliff—"above the level of a broadcast. But that did not help, not even when I straight-beamed . . ."

Blake could not straight-beam himself, but in the past he had been the recipient of such probes and he knew their force. Between twins such an aimed thought must be even more potent.

"Then," Marfy again shook the disk before his eyes, "this just kept on recording that everything was fine, blue sky and open land, as it were, all the way. This thing lied and is continuing to lie! And something *has* happened to Marva!"

"Could this be broken?" Blake fingered the disk. "Or hers?"

"I do not see how, they are warranted without a flaw. Wait!" She snatched at the locater that had led him from camp. "Now, let us see." She turned the gadget over in her hand, cupping it in her palm as she pressed a small button in its back case in a series of quick jabs. Having done so, she turned it over again so they could both see the dial.

The needle which had held so firmly toward the cliffs now swung loosely, came to a quivering stop, spun again when Marfy purposely shook her hand.

"Marva!" Her voice was a cry tinged with fear.

"What does that mean?" Blake's hand closed on the girl's shoulder to shake her gently as she still stared as if sight and mind were locked on the dial.

"She—she is not anywhere—not here!" Again Marfy feverishly shook the gadget, watched the needle spin in a crazy, purposeless whirl. "But she could not have—"

"Have what?"

"Gone off level! I was down there, right in the next room to the travel station, clear up to the moment when she lost mind touch. Our shuttle is at Vroom. There was no way for her to leave, and she would not have gone without telling me . . ."

There could be one other explanation, Blake knew, but he did not voice it aloud. Somewhere out in the stone wilderness there might lie a dead girl. Yet that beat he had heard—Marfy had said it was the proper reply for a disk worn by someone in no danger. In any event, there was trouble here right enough, and it was up to him to find out just what.

"A message . . ." Marfy thrust the locater into the front of her stormcoat. "I want to send a message to Com Varlt. Something has happened to Marva."

She started to run down the slope of the valley toward the camp, and Blake went pounding after her.

III

ONLY, THAT NEXT and important step was denied
them. For as they slipped and slid their way down
to the camp, Blake suddenly slowed to a stop. On
this time level where there was no need for concealment from native dwellers, installations were
boldly planted in the open. The energized rods
keeping communication channels open between
the Project and Vroom were beacon high—or had
been beacon high—against the sky. Now one
leaned at a sharp angle and the other, on the far
side of the camp, was not to be sighted at all!

But how . . . The importance of those would
have been so paramount to the men setting up the
camp that they would have based them firmly,
certainly made them secure against all assaults of
nature. Yet the unlikely happened.

Blake sloshed through a stream of muddy water
to the inclining pole. It was correctly set in rock,
but now a cavity had opened under that base,
undermining it. Blake frowned. He was no tech,
but the field men were neither stupid nor careless.
To choose a faulty base for a com rod was completely out of character. There would be an investigation of this when it was reported. And he
would have to do the reporting, in person.

"The rod is—" Marfy Rogan splashed to join
him.

"Useless. And I cannot see the other one, so that
may be down all the way. But how did they make
such an error in base sites?"

"Ask"—her reply was terse—"and perhaps you will also get an answer concerning personnel disks which do not work properly either!"

The laboring sound of a machine caused Blake to look around. One of the earth-movers he had seen crawling toward the flooded pens was now lumbering in their direction, the man in the driver's seat waving them out of the way. As Blake drew Marfy back, the mover clanked by and went to packing earth in an effort to keep the standard from falling to the ground.

Even if this one was righted and its fellow raised again, it would mean hours of delicate adjustment before they could once more be synchronized to open the message channel. And Blake wondered if there was any tech on the Project capable of such work. No, he would have to make his report in person and perhaps return with the men to do the job. And the sooner he got to it, the better. Still grasping Marfy's arm, he turned to the Headquarters shelter.

"You will be going back, won't you?" she asked. "Then I go, too."

"That is up to the Head, is it not?" Even part-time visitors to such a project were under the command of the Head. They took an oath agreeing to that before their passes were issued. Only a wardsman could come and go without any check from local authorities, acting under the orders of his own officers.

For the first time Blake saw her smile, a very fleeting one, "I do not think Isin Kutur will object. He will be only too glad to see the last of me. Unless . . ." She paused.

"Unless?"

"Unless he does not want my report on Marva to be heard."

"But why—" began Blake.

She turned on him, her expression one of scorn for his stupidity. "Limiters! This could be just the kind of story they would use. Marva lost in time . . ."

"But how can you be sure of that?" It seemed to Blake that she reached conclusions in a hasty fashion, none of them being more stably rooted than the rods of the camp.

"She is not in this world! Not anywhere!"

"But you said yourself that she had not, could not have, used the shuttle out of camp."

"Which simply means that somewhere, for some reason, there is another shuttle." Marfy was prompt with her answers, delivered in the firm tone of one who has made up her mind and intends to abide by it. "Oh, so you think that is impossible?" She flung the question at Blake, apparently reading his doubt in his expression. "It has happened before, you know that!"

It *had* happened before: illegal shuttles swinging from level to level, such as the one that had taken him on a nightmare journey of successor worlds on his first introduction to the crosstime activities of Vroom. But since then, security had so tightened that Blake could not believe any criminal or reckless, unlisted explorer might operate.

"I want to get to Com Varlt." Marfy pulled at Blake. "He will know what to do, how to reach Father."

"But who . . ." Even as he mumbled that, Blake was able to supply a few wild guesses himself: the

Limiters themselves, out to provoke some incident; illegal traders, though what would they
want on this world unless they had a cache here;
or an unauthorized explorer. Suppose that Marva
and the 'copter pilot had stumbled on something
not meant to be seen and accordingly had been
gathered in to suppress their discovery?

Against such an argument he could set the report of the 'copter pilot that he had found safe
shelter from the storm. That did not match such
suspicions.

However, one could not dismiss Marfy's dismay at the loss of mind touch. That could not be
tampered with, even if machine reports could be
altered. And according to her, the break in rapport
had come before the storm, before the pilot's report. And his own precognition . . . he could rely
on the truth of that even if it was only a general
warning. If he could only focus it, narrower it
would be more of a help.

"Who?" Marfy repeated. She spread out a hand,
spread her fingers, showing gray mud under the
nails. "I can give you several answers without
needing to search. But I want to start the hunt for
Marva." Her voice caught.

"All right. We can get back and—"

"Wardsman!" Kutur swung from the seat of
another machine and splashed heavily to meet
them at the entrance to Headquarters. The stocky
Head was smeared with mud, spatters of it freck-
ling his face when he had thrown back his hood.
"You see what has happened to the rods. Incompetence! Sheer incompetence! I shall report it.
You will take my tape back with you. I was assured of complete cooperation, and what do I get?

Incompetence from those upon whom our safety depends! And"—he swung to Marfy as if he saw her for the first time—"reckless disregard for orders on the part of silly young females who have no business being here in the first place! Pass or no pass, girl, you return now to Vroom!"

"And Marva?" Marfy's voice was a little shrill as she interrupted him.

"And Marva also. Once Garglos returns her to this camp, she will be sent after you. No more will I have to deal with foolishness!"

"When Garglos and Marva return," Marfy persisted. "And when will that be, Head Kutur, and where shall they return from?"

He stared at her as if she were babbling utter nonsense. "They will return from a field flight and very soon, if Garglos follows orders, which hitherto he has done. As to where they are coming from, it is Sector Dot One, as you well know, girl"

Marfy shook her head. "Marva went off level this morning before the storm, a complete time unit before."

Kutur swung his head slowly, not as an answer to her words but as if that simple gesture would clear away some fog of thinking. "What are you saying, girl? Nonsense, all of it. You, yourself, saw your sister leave in the 'copter. Level-hopping, is it? Stupid nonsense!" He tapped the disk on his belt. "This tells us that all is well with her. Why do you mouth so wild a tale?"

"I do not care what that says!" Marfy retorted. "I lost mind touch and that I do believe. Marva went off level, and if your gadgets say otherwise, then they lie!"

Kutur's face reddened, his shoulders hunched,

his hands came up, the fingers working a little.

"You!" he exploded at Blake, "get her away, get her away from here. Two pens utterly lost, the rods down, and now this raving to listen to. A man can take only so much! Take her back with you. I do not ask that, I order it! I will listen to no more. And when her sister returns, she will be sent also to Vroom."

"When do you expect the 'copter back?" Blake asked. "The shuttle is a small one, but for a nonstop run, I can wait and take them both."

"Wait?" Kutur's lips puffed in an explosion of breath and word together. "You do not wait when I say go! I want techs here, those rods up again, we do not know how many storms lie ahead. It is not beyond reasonable belief that we may have to build from the beginning again. What can be saved now, must be. Go at once!"

"Head," Scylias stood in the doorway behind his superior, "Forkus reports no hour signal from the 'copter. He used both short and extended beam."

For a second or two it was as if Kutur did not hear his assistant, and Blake watched the other closely. If the Head was expecting such news, he could not guess it by the reaction that followed. Because Kutur went into swift action.

Under a volley of orders the second of the Project's small air-exploration flyers was wheeled out. Blake shed the cumbersome stormcoat and reached the door of its cabin on the heels of the pilots, who was, in this instance, Kutur himself. The Head glowered at the wardsman.

"What do you—"

Blake cut him short, sure of his own authority in

this instance. "I am responsible for—" he began.

Kutur snorted. "Get in, get in, do not waste time reciting your duties and virtues. If you linger about to use your tongue, you may be responsible for things you will not wish, wardsman!"

They were airborne almost before Blake made fast the door. Kutur had a heavy hand on the controls, bouncing the light craft up, half-jerking Blake out of his seat. Then they were heading at maximum speed away from the valley camp.

Kutur appeared to know just where he was going, and the broken, rocky terrain of the cliffs sped below them as they left the valley. Volcanic action in the past was evident and Blake thought it would be close to impossible to comb that territory at ground level. But with the 'copter they covered long stretches of it.

Another river passed beneath them, this one encased in a sharply walled gorge. The water was broken by white lacing on the rock-tattered flood. Now they lifted again to a plateau with further heights of mountain to the east. Kutur slacked speed, circling and finally touching down with a back-wracking bounce on relatively smooth surface.

Once there he did not display any great desire to leave the flyer, but hunched forward in his seat, peering through the windbreak at the beginning slopes of the mountains. Blake had his hand on the door latch, but he was determined not to leave the cabin without Kutur. His sense continued to warn him, though as yet without the sharp thrust signaling immediate peril.

"Well?" He broke the silence when the Head continued to sit there. "Which way now?"

"There!" The other pointed. "It should be sheltered under that ledge."

He was right in so much: a ledge overhung a space which might be large enough to shelter a twin to the flyer they now occupied. But if the other 'copter had been there, it was now gone. The rock was bare, like all the rest of this wilderness.

"This—this I do not believe. Look you!" Kutur's hand shot out. Held rigid between thumb and forefinger was the personnel disk from his belt. "This says that they are safe, all is well. The locater brings us along the beam to here. Yet there is nothing!"

"They could already have lifted to return to camp," Blake suggested.

"But no." Kutur pounded his fist on his knee. "There would be no reason for them not to fly straight to camp, and if they had been airborne we should have seen them. Also, they would have answered signals. Do not tell me that they have sunk into this rock. That I will not believe!"

"That was wild country over which we passed, a wreck there . . ." Blake made himself say that.

"There was no automatic distress call broadcast." Kutur shook his head. "These," again he flourished the disk, "these do not lie. All my time on Project, many projects, in places where danger ever stalked at one's heels, lying in wait, these have been our safeguards. Yet now this one says what our eyes tell us is false. I do not understand, none of this do I understand." His bewilderment was complete; he had lost his arrogance and self-assurance.

Without knowing what he was looking for, save the vague chance that some sign of the lost 'copter might indeed remain, Blake left the flyer and walked slowly into the shadow of the ledge. The storm had left pools in rock pockets and now the hot sun was already steaming them away. No chance of any tracks. A small suspicion pricked at Blake. In spite of Kutur's certainty, he was not sure that this was where the others had been.

A scratch on the stone, anything . . . Suppose Marfy was right and an illegal shuttle *was* in use? For one of those, there need be no such terminal as existed at camp. If its user had a travel code, was sure of an open surface for a breakthrough, he could land anywhere.

The pocket sheltered by the ledge was larger than it appeared from the flyer. The pilot of the other 'copter would have had no difficulty in running in during the storm. And—Blake went down on one knee, rubbed his finger along a scored line—that was no natural scratch and it was fresh. So . . . the 'copter might reasonably be supposed to have been here. That being so, where was it now? Any illegal shuttle—Blake's thoughts continue to return to that—would not be of a size to take aboard a flyer. Or, his imagination soared again, was there an outward trader in operation with a shuttle designed to handle cargo, perhaps operating between successor worlds and not from Vroom at all?

"What is it?" Kutur had followed, stooped to examine the scratch as Blake moved on to search the rest of the area.

"Sign that they might have been here, but nothing else."

"Here, yes. I know that! But where have they gone? Tell me that. Garglos—he is not a boy, he does not play. He does not say he will do one thing, go in one direction, and then change his mind. Garglos is a man to be depended upon. I know him. He has worked with me for years. So why is he missing? And why do these lie and tell me that he is as usual?" Again Kutur held out the personnel disk and shook it fiercely.

"But," he took control of himself, "this is not good. We can do nothing here. One does not claw answers out of rocks with one's fingernails."

"You have detectors, persona beams?" Blake cut in. "Use them for an air search."

Kutur nodded. "There is nothing else to be done. Since we can no longer depend, it would seem, upon the devices which have always served us in such cases, then, yes, we shall turn to the general alarm system. But we are not equipped with highpowered detectors. Those must be brought from wardsmen's depots. And without the rods—"

"Someone takes the message in person," Blake completed. "All right, get me back to camp, and I am on my way to do just that."

During the trip back to Project Headquarters, Kutur was sunk in thought which, to judge by his thunderous expression, was of the darkest. As they climbed from the flyer, he spoke for the first time.

"We shall rig a makeshift and search the best we can. But be you quick, also, wardsman. You have seen this country; this is a dead world. Water, yes, it is drinkable, will keep life going for awhile. But there is nothing else out there to preserve a man on foot, injured. They would have very little chance."

No hint that Kutur had any suspicions of an illegal shuttle. He was now obviously ready to believe in a wilderness crash as he had denied that possibility before. But too many things did not add up for Blake. The message from Garglos that he had his machine and presumably his passenger, Marva Rogan, in shelter. Yet that had come some time after Marfy's rapport with her sister had been broken . . . and Blake's own personal warning. He must get Com Varlt on this, and quickly!

"You did not find them." A flat statement of fact and not a question. Marfy waited just inside the Headquarters door.

Kutur shook his head. "Ulad," he pushed past her to call, "take the detector from the crawler, it must be mounted on the 'copter—"

Marfy caught at Blake's arm. "The detector?" Her voice was hardly above a thin whisper. "Could they have crashed—out there?"

Blake could not conceal what she had already guessed from Kutur's order. "It is possible . . ."

But she was shaking her head. "I know that Marva is not in this world, I knew it as soon as she left. But she did not leave it that way. Death or injury to her—I would feel it with her!" Her voice was still very low as if her words were aimed only at Blake. "You—you found no sign of anything else?"

"Of a shuttle?" Blake matched his tone to hers. "No, but any outlawed level-hopper would not have a permanent base such as this."

Marfy's reason for her conclusion concerning her sister's disappearance made better sense the longer Blake considered it. A mental bond ended by death could not be mistaken by the one who shared it. He had no personal experience of telepathic union, but when such was strengthened by close relationship and emotional ties, Blake knew it was a very deep and enduring form of communication. Had Marva died out there, Marfy, in a way, would also have suffered a taste of death, and she would have known the truth in that instant.

"Com Varlt." She pulled at his sleeve. "If she was taken to another level, the sooner he knows the better."

With that Blake was in full agreement. Kutur had rallied the rest of the Project; there was a great deal of hurrying to and fro. With the rods down, Blake's own duty was to report in and in person. Marfy was hurrying him along, pulling at him.

"Come on!" she demanded impatiently.

They went, apparently attracting no attention from the others, to the shuttle. A return course had been automatically set before the transferer had left Vroom and locked in. Sometimes such a return might be a hurried one, dictated by attack, accident, or the need for moving a wardsman unable to function with either mind or body in the best of condition. Still Blake followed procedure and checked the code, while Marfy strapped in on the companion seat.

The dials were correct as he expected. He pressed the release lever. The swirl of time-exit caught them; they were bemused momentarily by the disorientation of the pass-through.

"How long?" Marfy asked as Blake turned his head to see her.

"An hour, a little more."

But he had no more than said that than his eyes blurred; the spin once more pressed him against the cushions of the seat. But—the trip surely could not be over!

The cabin was tilting, sliding. Save for the belts that bound them to their seats, they would have been flung against its side as the shuttle started a tobogganing progress to the left.

IV

WHEN THEY CAME to a halt, the cabin was tilted at a sharp angle, and it shook ominously when Blake moved. His first attention was for the control panel. The small light signifying that they were on a successor world and not in passage was on. For the rest, the Vroom code was clearly visible.

"What—what happened?"

"Don't move!" Blake ordered. Under them the shuttle was rocking as if it sat delicately balanced on the edge of a drop.

With infinite care Blake loosed his safety belt. Then he inched forward to press the button for the emergency viewplate so that he could see beyond the suddenly unstable cabin.

Green! A thick wall of green, so blazing in color that it took him a second or two to detect individual leaves, bits of broken branches, ground against the viewport. What had happened or where they were, Blake had no idea. But that they were neither at the Project camp nor in a ward depot, he knew.

Blake slammed his flattened palm against the lying course code. Blandly the same figures continued to show. And the shuttle shuddered.

"We—we are sliding again!"

Marfy was right. The cabin lurched and began another sidewise slip. Blake clung to his seat as the movement quickened.

"Your head," he gasped at his companion. "Get it down! We may land hard!"

He balled himself as well as he could in the

padded seat. The girl followed his example, and he had a flash of relief that she had not become hysterical. Only this much he was sure of—they had not landed at any regular stop.

The impact at the end of that slide was not as severe as Blake had feared. The tilt of the cabin was less acute and there was a bouncing sensation, as if the shuttle had come to rest on some elastic surface which cushioned it. Once more Blake looked to the viewplate.

Green again, but this time, also, a palm-sized piece of blue sky. Blake drew a deep breath and turned to observe Marfy Rogan. She dropped the protecting circle of her arm to blink back at him.

"We—we are not at a depot—a real one, are we?" Her voice was a monotone as if she struggled to keep control over a boiling surge of emotion. Her face, still showing here and there a freckle of storm mud on her clear skin, wore a rigid, set expression.

"That much we can be sure of." Blake moved experimentally. There was no answering tremor in the cabin; they had reached some form of stability.

"How . . ." she began again.

Blake shook his head impatiently. "No idea. This is still set"—for the second time he gave the location device a sharp rap—"on Vroom."

He got to his feet, taking each step with caution. He pressed two buttons, then the panel lifted free so that he could see what lay behind.

Blake stiffened. The panel had hidden disaster: fused wiring, a tangled mass of installation so completely ruined that perhaps only a first-rank tech could ever make sense of it again! Behind the set code someone had deliberately made chaos of the most important part of the shuttle—its directional guide.

"You—you cannot fix it?" That was more plea than question.

"No." Blake could not change that curt negative. "I do not think anyone could outside a shop."

"Then we are lost." Marfy still sat in her seat, her hands resting on its padded arms. Her fingers clenched the supports so that the knuckles were sharp knobs under the thin skin.

"We have the emergency call." Blake turned away from the ruined direction installation. Unless, he thought, that has been sabotaged too. Of course the call was short range. Perhaps all they could contact was the Project. Which was worse than useless, for with the rods out and no second shuttle—plus the fact that they might well have landed on an unexplored world for which no code existed—they would have no help from that direction. Extreme luck might present an alternative, a roving patroller near enough to pick up a distress signal, if the apparatus to send such remained operative.

Blake went straight to the panel behind the sender. It took a bit of prying, but he got it off. At least to the eye there was nothing wrong here, no discernible damage. So, partially assured, he rigged a routine distress signal.

"If this is a coded level," Marfy's voice was still strained, "then . . ."

"Then we have to supply some identification," he told her.

They were close to the Project level; the time

element of their interrupted trip argued that. There was a series of successor worlds at this end of the crosstime swing, none of them too well-known until one reached the Forest level. But perhaps that would be in their favor, too—there was a steady stream of traffic in that direction—if they were close enough for their call to register.

Contact was only the first step though. If they could not give a coordinate to code this level, and with the director so eviscerated that was impossible, then they would have to provide clues so the experts could "set" their present whereabouts in the master pattern at Headquarters. And all this would take time, more time than he cared to dwell upon.

Of course, there would also be a follow-up when Blake did not return on schedule from the run to the Project. No message from him would lead to a trip and a general alarm. Then the hunt would be up. But they had to provide a clue to the right world.

"How—how can we tell them?" Marfy's thoughts had followed a similar road.

"Type of vegetation, landmarks, anything that will give an expert a chance to 'set' it," Blake replied. That meant he must do some exploring outside the safety of the cabin. He must take view-shots of everything out there that held any promise of being identifiable and then send them through on call, if and when they had an answer to that. But at least Marfy would have occupation to keep her busy, tending that very necessary link with their only hope of escape.

As Blake coded the distress signal and set it on as wide a range band as he could force the machine to take, he explained what must be done.

"Then you are going out there?"

"We have to have views to send through when you pick up an acceptance. Those will help in identification."

If their signal was picked up, *if* he could find some level identification—if, if, if! Blake went to one of the emergency lockers and unrolled an exploration kit.

There was the thin suit, hood, mask, which, when donned over his coveralls, would give him protection from insect attack, disease, low radiation. The viewer he slung by its cord to rest on his chest, and he added one of the needlers, a weapon which shot darts tipped with a narcotic to stupefy any attacker but do no eventual harm.

Marfy watched him silently. But when his hand was on the hatch lock, she spoke. "What if something happens to you out there?"

Blake tapped the com disk set into the mask of his hood. "I am going to keep reporting all the time. It must be taped for recast when you pick up a contact. And you will hear it. Armed with this"—he showed the needler—"I have nothing really to fear. Now . . ."

She raised her hand. "Good luck!"

Blake smiled at her. "We have had fairly good fortune already. This may have been a rocky landing but we came out in one piece. And that luck may continue to hold. You call while I explore."

He was using the double hatch now, just in case. Having carefully dogged the inner portal into place, he squeezed around to face the outer. The chamber was a very narrow fit, but it spelled safety in some worlds where the atmosphere was poisoned or there was suspicion of radiation, and wardsmen did not take chances.

Beyond the outer door lay a clean scar in the soil, cut deep into the red earth and fringed by broken and torn vegetation, leading up a rather steep slope, the mark of their skidding. Blake studied that and began dictating distances as well as he could judge them. The difference between their present resting place and where they had broken into this successor world would have a vital bearing on the code. And it was the first fact he had to give.

Digging both feet and hands into the slippery soil, Blake fought his way up the ridge to where they must have first emerged into this level. By the signs, they had materialized on the very edge of the drop, over-balanced, and slid into a small ravine. There a heavy growth of brush acted as a cushion for their landing.

Just as the Project had been rooted on a bare spread of rock, here was a tangled wealth of green. It was humid, hot, full of life. Huge insects soared, buzzed over the broken moss left by the shuttle's descent. Some were butterflies, their six- and eight-inch wings a brilliant riot of color. Others were slim of body and wing, moving with a buzzing whirr. Pressing the button of his view-taker, as well as describing the scene orally, Blake recorded such scenery and examples of native life as were in range. The majority of the larger growth was fernlike, some fronds rising to the dignity of trees. There was a flash of scarlet as something about as high as his waist darted from one mass of foliage to another. Its speed of movement made it a blur to his eyes, and Blake could not determine its nature save that he retained a strong impression it had scurried on two feet. The hiding place it had darted into was on the steepest portion of the slope and he refrained from hunting it there.

Behind the crest of the drop down which they had gone was a heavily wooded strip of reasonably flat country, then cliffs again, not too different from those that had walled in the valley of the Project. In fact, if one stripped away the vegetation, the contours of this country, Blake decided, resembled those of the sterile world. The ravine into which the shuttle had toppled could mark part of the river valley. Only he did not hear the sound of the sea; and when he faced west, he could see no trace of the restless ocean, unless a creamy line along the very rim of the horizon marked the sand of distant beaches.

Again Blake caught a corner-eye view of swift movement and turned to survey the spot where that red flicker had been. Not even a trembling of leaf or twig betrayed what might have taken cover there. But his danger sense was alert, and Blake was as sure as if he had been forewarned that he was now the focal point for action to come. Stalked? Why? By what?

If he could reach the top of the cliff, he might get a better view of the countryside. But to do so meant forcing a path through thick undergrowth, and Blake was sure that that stretch of green was not devoid of life. He studied the thickets before him intently, striving to pick out the easiest breakthrough.

Still dictating, pausing now and then for a view shot, he pressed on into a fern patch which brushed about him almost waist high. He swung with vigor another explorer's tool, a keen-edged, broad-bladed knife the length of his forearm, cutting an opening, careful to toss the slashed leaves and branches to one side so he could see the ground he cleared. Yet all the time he knew that he was under observation, that there was, in this miniature fern forest, that which flickered at high speed away from his path when detection seemed imminent, only to keep pace with him.

Blake had not anticipated such action from animals. This continued and the cunning surveillance was disturbing. Twice he turned up the audio plates of his hood, striving to catch any sound of hidden pursuit. The buzz of insects, sharp cries which appeared to be from a greater distance, and the regular clunk of his machete against stems, the rustle of the leaves he threw aside, were all he heard.

For some reason the passage seemed to take a long time. And, though the physical action was moderate, Blake was sweating when he came to the foot of the cliff wall. This was rough but not so pitted with climbing holds as the one at the Project. He edged westward along its base, hunting the best ascent, and finally found a possible one.

Turning back the attached gloves of the suit, Blake began the pull up the barrier. When he reached the top, he tumbled over into another fern bed, crushing the fronds under him as he squirmed around to look back, bringing out his distance lenses. The shuttle was a silver coin, resting, not quite level, in the ravine. And that did hide water at its lowest point, for now he had glimpses of a wandering stream. And he had been right in his guess about the distant ocean, for the glasses brought the billows of dunes closer when he faced due west.

On turning the glasses south, he discovered that his vantage point allowed him to scan another valley where ran a river as broad as and seemingly like the one that housed Kutur's pens. Flats of mud banked it on both sides. But those flats—Blake stiffened. No whim of nature had ever thrown up those divisions, marked by low stone walls, on the stretches of mud. No, those had been erected for a purpose and with intelligence behind that purpose. And they lined the flats on both sides of the river as far as Blake's lenses made clear.

There was this further oddity. The divisions were all three-sided, with the portions facing the stream left unwalled. And now he made out another strange thing: at the river side of each of those three-sided fields—if fields they could be termed—there was another stone, very large, standing alone. On the river face of those near him he could see markings, lines without meaning. Yet the markings on each stone differed from those of its neighbor. Blake put a telelens on the viewer and took shots of all within registering distance.

The fields, the marking stones, the river. There was nothing else to be seen. No green of plant showed on the mud stretches. If the walled fields were intended for crop cultivation, this was either not the right season or all those farms were deserted, no longer in use.

In two of the nearer fields, close to the river, were platforms of piled stone and earth, their upper surfaces level. And from the water's edge to these led ramps of packed earth.

As Blake sighted on one of these with his

viewer, there was a ripple in the slow-moving
water, veeing against the current, then turning to
head out of the water, moving ponderously but
with vast dignity. A big head raised, the arch of a
dripping carapace was fully revealed in the sun
and what was now late afternoon.

The turtle must have been close to five feet in
diameter, Blake estimated. Its shell displayed an
elaborate design of raised whorls. The general
color was a dark brown, but the scaled legs and
the head were patterned with vivid yellow and
red markings. And the head was the strangest of
all. Far too large ever to be withdrawn for safety
within the shell after the fashion of its species, it
was equipped with a kind of shield shaped not
unlike a broad spearhead, the point jutting out
over the nose, the rest spreading wide and back to
the shell.

Having pulled up on the ramp, the creature
made a deliberate climb to the platform, and then
turned about to face the cliff where Blake stood.
Since its field of vision was of necessity limited by
its head armament, Blake did not trouble to take
cover but continued to run the viewer.

The longer he watched, the more the differences between this shelled monster and the turtles of his own knowledge were manifest. And its
movements also mystified him. It raised one huge
foot, armed with clearly visible claws, and then
the other in turn to its mouth. Having done so
twice, it rested.

But it was not alone for long. From the very foot
of the cliff below Blake's perch shot scarlet
streaks, darting toward the platform in the field.
They did not mount the dais, but gathered at its

foot, their crested heads all upturned, their wide jaws a little agape as they stared back at the helmed turtle.

Lizards, save that their body-covering seemed more skin than plate or scales, vividly scarlet. A series of spike excrescences gave them nearly uniform topknots. And—Blake clicked tongue against teeth— His taped words might not be given credence but the viewer would back him up: each of those red warriors trailed a polished spear, barbed with a wicked-looking point!

About to attack the turtle? No, they continued to crouch before the larger creature's platform. The reptile might almost be a general reviewing troops, though the lizards did not indulge in any marching display. In fact, as far as Blake could see, they did nothing at all but squat and stare up at the platform.

There was, after several long moments, more action. One of the lizards broke from the company of its fellows, was off in a flashing dart of speed. Weaving a way around the field walls, heading up the river valley. It could have been a messenger in search of reinforcements. Yet the rest of the troop made no move to surround the platform, or to lay siege to the ramp down which the turtle might escape into the river.

Another darting streak of red, this time toward Blake's cliff. And that was followed, seconds later, by a larger pack of its companions, while the turtle continued to rest motionless and apparently uncaring.

Blake's special sense alerted him. He shoved the lenses into the carrying case, swung around just as one of the small spears flashed through the air and was turned aside by his explorer's suit. This was only the first of a rain of spears thudding against him to clatter down about his feet. While he had been watching the actions of one company of the scarlet lizard spearmen, it was clear that a second one had attacked him from the rear.

Though his suit continued to turn those weapons, Blake did not greatly fancy the descent into the valley of the shuttle while under fire. He could not return fire with the needler, for his attackers snapped into view, loosed their weapons, and were out of sight at a rate of speed he could not match. He might not be as slow as the turtle, but neither was he lizard-swift.

"Blake!" Marfy broke silence for the first time since he had left her. "Blake! The shuttle is moving!"

He threw himself at the cliff edge. To have the machine suddenly take on life while he was gone . . . Perhaps its broken coder would hurl it into another world—if that was possible! After what had happened to so-called accident-proof installations, he could believe anything *was* possible.

"Level-hopping?" He demanded to know as he lowered himself to the first handholds.

"No, it is moving here, along the ground," came her answer, in one way a reassurance to quiet his overwhelming fear. He paused to look for himself.

Marfy was right. The shuttle was moving, slowly and jerkily but moving, westward in the general direction of the distant seashore. A spear struck close to his right hand, too close. Blake put on speed, intent upon reaching the valley floor. Now he could hear the rustling in the bushes made by those who were still pushing the attack, fruitless as it had been so far.

V

BLAKE TOOK the path he had hacked at a dead run. And so almost came to disaster, for he had barely time to see the barricade heaped in the narrow lane to entangle his feet before he was upon it. He leaped that, again meeting a rain of spears that rattled against the protective covering about his thighs and body. Now he heard an angry, sibilant hissing, the battle cries of his enemies.

The wardsman burst from the thick vegetation, came to the scar caused by the downward path of the shuttle. The silvery oval machine was moving westward at a slow pace, and from above he could sight no reason for that. It was as if the ground under the machine was in motion. Yet well before the bulk of the shuttle struck them, branches bent, cracked, went down to clear a path.

"Blake!" Marfy's voice sounded in his earphones.

"I am here, just above you . . ."

"Blake, they are telepathic!"

"Who?" he demanded as he angled down the slope, wanting to reach a point ahead of that weird procession of invisible road clearers and the moving shuttle.

"I cannot read them, they are on a band too low. But they consider us an enemy they have been expecting. Fear and hate—that much comes through."

If the most effective weapons this world's natives had were the spears Blake had already met, he and Marfy had nothing to fear. But to be moved too far from the shuttle's point of entry into this

level was another and more potent danger. Blake
slid to the bow of the crawling machine, managed
to get a closer look at what was happening there.
For one or two startled seconds he thought that
his first impression was right, that the earth itself
was rolling under the shuttle, oversetting the
bushes rooted in it to insure passage of the alien
machine. Then he was aware of the truth.

Turtles or tortoises—Blake knew that there was
a difference but he was hazy as to what comprised
it—were moving with deliberation but with concentrated determination, using their bulk to
smash down and flatten the growth. There were at
least six of them, massive, shelled creatures although smaller than the giant he had watched
crawl out of the river and differing from it in other
ways. Their shells were not so corrugated, and
their feet and heads were yellow-brown and not
vividly striped.

As the shuttle lurched forward another foot,
Blake caught a glimpse of a horny leg thrust forward from beneath it to get a fresh hold. And he
guessed that the craft must rest on the backs of an
unknown number of turtles who were thus transporting it in their own fashion.

Such group effort could argue only one of two
things: efficient training or intelligence itself in
action. Wardsman instruction had prepared Blake
for an open-minded acceptance of strange sights
and action on any successor world. In a thousand
alternate times man had servants, tools, friends,
which were alive but of a different species. Was it
so hard to accept that here turtles and lizards were
so used? Yet . . .

The lizards were armed and Marfy had discovered a telepathic contact which was alien,

whereas any human brain would be—or should be—open to her. No shield had discouraged communication; there had just been a clear difference in thought-range.

Blake squatted on his heels as the shuttle crawled into a relatively open space. He was right! The machine rested on the shells of a number of tortoises. One dropped out and another, one of those clearing the path, fell back to take its place. Purposeful effort.

A spear struck Blake's shoulder and clattered to the ground. His lizard escort was still in action. Now, to get at him, they had to come into the open. Blake snapped a needle shot at one slim scarlet figure drawing itself up to launch a weapon. And he was lucky, for the needle struck in the upraised arm of the reptile. It made a convulsive leap in the air, hissed, and then tumbled limply down the slope where Blake gathered it up.

Instantly a rain of spears fell about him. But he paid no attention as he fired at the slowly moving tortoise legs. He planted two darts before the shuttle shuddered to a stop; the legs which had provided his targets, pulled back into their shell protection. But, like the river turtle, this band of crawlers could not retract their over-large heads. So Blake found the targets he needed in throat and neck. He was never quite sure how many were concerned in that feat of transportation. But he continued to fire until they were all quiet. Then, carrying his lizard captive—he would have liked one of the tortoises in addition but he had neither the strength nor the equipment to move it—Blake entered the cabin.

Together with Marfy he examined the slender

body. Standing on its hind legs, as they appeared to prefer locomotion, the creature was about four feet tall. It was not scaled but covered with a soft, rough skin. Nor was it uniformly scarlet; the skin bore dark markings in complicated patterns here and there. The ragged-looking topknot was hard to the touch as if, under the skin, there was some bone projection. By its lack of teeth, having only bony ridges within its jaws, they guessed it to be non-carnivorous.

"Look!" Marfy stooped to touch what hung about its neck. A cord of plaited stuff which might have been either grass or skin string, and on it a small oval of bone. Scratched deeply into that were two lines like those Blake had recorded from the river field-marker stone. For the rest, the captive could have been a wild creature.

"Turtles!" Marfy echoed when Blake told her of the motive power that had been moving the shuttle to an unknown destination.

"Turtles and armed lizards. And what is behind it or who is behind it is anyone's guess," Blake continued. "How about the distress call?"

"On, for the widest sweep. But, Blake, do you realize we have broken the first law?"

The first law of crosstime: no revelation of their presence to any natives of any time level, unless it was also possible to give that native a false memory.

"Not the first time it has happened," Blake commented, "and we had no choice. You can't contact them at all? Try."

Marfy closed her eyes as if to concentrate the better. There was a chance, if they could establish telepathic communication with a higher intelligence, they might find aid or at least make sure there would be no more attempts to take them away from their point of entry.

Blake watched the girl. Though her face lacked expression, he could sense the effort she was putting into that search. Then her eyes opened.

"Nothing, now just nothing at all!"

"You mean they have gone out of range of your band?"

"No, before I could catch them they wove in and out of my lowest range. It was unintelligible, but now there is utter silence. They—or it—are not broadcasting at all."

Blake turned to the viewport. There was a scarlet blot on the hillside marking a gathering of lizards. Even as he watched, they launched their weapons at the shuttle. But the machine was immobile; the turtles lay in drugged sleep and would continue so for some hours. The turtles—could they be the intelligences Marfy had picked up before?Intelligent turtles? He made that a vocal protest.

However, Marfy did not seem startled. "Why not? This is perhaps a world in which mankind did not develop at all. There are many of those worlds and we have not begun to explore them. What dispute can we make if another species did develop intelligence and rule nature here? Turtles are long-lived. These have abnormally large heads, perhaps more brain power than their kind ever carried on any level wherein man dwells. They are very old as a species, too, for they lived among the great reptiles before the first mammal walked the earth. Blake, this is a wonderful discovery, one that will be famous!"

If we ever get a chance to report it, Blake thought. And then, seeing the faint change of expression on her face, he knew that she shared his thought.

"Turtles, and you say they marked us down for enemies?"

"The shape of the shuttle—perhaps it looks like a giant of their own species and they were taking it prisoner," she hazarded.

"But what of these?" Blake picked up the limp lizard. The skin was not chill as he expected reptilian flesh to feel, but warm and velvety.

"Slow movers might go into partnership with another species which possesses quicker reactions. Perhaps this is a pet, a servant, or a comrade-in-arms. What are you going to do with it?"

"Take a reading, then restore it to its friends. What else?" Blake arranged the body carefully on a pull-out shelf and centered the viewer on it. The record would not be as complete as that of a laboratory report, but enough to give the authorities a good idea of this particular inhabitant of a hitherto unknown world. When Blake was done, he went out to lay the unconscious lizard on a pile of bracken the turtles had thrown to one side. He took time to inspect the still sleeping shelled ones. As far as he could determine there were no signs of their rousing, and Blake hoped that that would continue.

When he returned, he discovered that Marfy had brought out ration packs and was opening them. But Blake picked up half to stow away again.

"Sorry—" he began, but she nodded quickly.

"I know, we must be careful. Maybe I *am* as foolish as Head Kutur says. Drink?" She had snapped off the lid of a self-heating can of stimulating drink. At Blake's gesture she sipped several times before passing it on.

"I have been thinking." Now she nibbled at one of the unappetizing but very nutritious cakes of combinerac.

"About turtles?" he encouraged as she hesitated. Inwardly Blake was amazed at what he considered Marfy Rogan's fortitude. He knew very little about the women of her class in Vroom, but those he had seen and met at official functions had always seemed beings wrapped in luxury, very carefully sheltered by their men. For a long time in Vroom, after the atomic disasters of the distant past had nearly wiped out the total population of that successor world, men had outnumbered women. The survivors had been mainly in concealed military installations or in small mixed groups that had found refuge underground or those who had scattered to distant parts of the earth.

Radiation had given rise to mutations in the very small succeeding generation. Many of these had not survived, but others had. And then had followed the development of psi powers which set the people of Vroom on other paths of exploration, both mental and physical. The need for women had sparked the first trips crosstime after the discovery of such travel had been made. For a time Vroom men had recruited wives from other levels. Then that had been made a crime, carrying the penalty of complete mental erasure.

The women of Vroom were cherished. Few of

them ever crosstimed, unless to safe levels for
family holidays or as members of research teams
such as in the Project they had just left. Blake
knew of no instance in which women had visited
an inhabited level in disguise as the wardsmen
and traders did. So he was astounded at Marfy's
quick adjustment to their present predicament.

"I have been thinking," she began once more,
"about Marva. How did she get off-level? By an
outlaw hopper? Could she and Garglos have seen
such in action? Such a barren world would be a
good one on which to set up a cache."

His own speculation put into words. "The 'copter vanished, too," he mused.

"Or seemed to," she broke in. "The passengers
could be kidnapped, the flyer dropped down a
river gorge or something of the sort. And
then"—her eyes fell almost as if she did not want
to say what was in her mind before she added with
a rush—"Marva might be persuaded into—into an
adventure."

"What do you mean?"

"You are lucky, Blake Walker." She was looking at him now and there was a blaze in her eyes,
green-blue eyes the color of the ocean he had seen
in his own world. "There are no doors closed to
you, no one lets you listen to descriptions of all
the wonders of crosstime and then refuses to let
you view them for yourself! All my life I have
listened to tapes, seen views of successor worlds,
heard all the stories such people as Com Varlt and
my father have to tell. But am I allowed a story of
my own or to see for myself? No!"

"You are doing both now," Blake commented
dryly, "and under circumstances anyone but a

trained wardsman is usually protected from experiencing."

"Yes. I know all the warnings and the sensible reasons behind the rules. Those have been dinned into my ears for years. But suppose it is also in me not to be contented, a stay-at-home daughter of a Hundred family? Suppose I want to go crosstime so much it sometimes seems that wishing is a real pain? Well, that is true. And it is also true of Marva. And she likes rules and orders even less than I. Many times I have been able to talk her out of the foolishness of breaking those rules. Supposing she was given a chance to do so once when I was not there?"

"You believe she would level-hop voluntarily if offered the chance for what seemed like an adventure?"

Marfy answered that by her expression, leading Blake to explore new lines of speculation. Offered a short hop to be made secretly, Marva might accept, and perhaps then find herself a captive of her companions on another successor world. But that made it even more possible she was in the hands of an outlaw. For a woman to turn up at the legal depot on any successor world where a legitimate wardsman team was in control would mean instant exposure and arrest.

And tracing an outlaw crosstime—unconsciously Blake shook his head. He had taken part in such a wild hunt before. And he knew the time, energy, and the need for luck such a quest entailed. Meanwhile, the search could never begin unless their own luck took a big step from dark to light.

"If I wanted to interest Marva past the limit of

prudence," Marfy gazed past Blake into space, "I would mention World E625."

Blake shook his head. No wardsman could keep track of the successor worlds in entirety. Before any crosstime patrol he was given intensive briefing on those he would visit. Blake could recall out of his own past experiences those on which he personally had been caught up in some piece of action. He would remember all his life the three worlds to which the spinning shuttle of the outlaw Pranj had carried him. But outside of such specific information, one had to apply to the general file at Headquarters.

"Last year we saw the special viewing of the commercial team from there. Marva talked about it for months. Level E625—I would know at once."

"You?"

Marfy nodded briskly. "Yes. You can't just go in and pick up someone, not if they have been purposely hidden. But once I reach the successor world where Marva is, I can beam her and learn just how to reach her. There is no one or any machine that can do that. So I will have to go."

Blake did not attempt to argue with her. If she wished to spend the present laying fantastic plans for the future, he had no quarrel with that. But the fact that they might never get a chance to put those plans or any other intentions into action did not appear to worry her in the least. That fact was forbiddingly plain to Blake.

He went to the call unit. It beamed in regular pulsations, sending their appeal for help flooding out, though whether their slide down the cliff and the subsequent alteration of site made by the determined turtles had dislocated it past an effective sending he could not be sure. From the viewplate he could see the hillside. The massed scarlet of the lizards had vanished. Either they had given up their determined attack on the shuttle or had moved out of range of the viewer. There was nothing, absolutely nothing, to be done now but wait. Outside the coming of evening was defined by the dimming of light and the lengthening of shadows.

Blake slung the chairs into recline position. Marfy settled in one but sat up again as Blake switched off the cabin illumination.

"Why?"

"No use attracting any attention in the dark," he explained. From their window plate that light could ray as a beacon.

"But if help comes, they could not see us."

"We will know if they are coming through. Time enough then to light up." Blake centered his attention on the alarm that would make that true. As time passed, their chances grew slimmer, fraction by fraction. Of course, authorities would send a patrol through to the Project. Then his own shuttle would be certified as lost—*if* the second patroller was not also sabotaged.

What *was* happening on the Project level that caused some member of the team there to take such a fantastic step? Or were the Rogan girls the focus of all the trouble?

Blake could go on, spinning any number of reasons, most of them highly improbable, and maybe never hit on the right one at all. The cabin suddenly shifted again. He heard an exclamation from Marfy.

"The turtles?"

Could he go out there in the dark and use the needler with any accuracy, armed with only a torch? Resignedly Blake, scrambling out of his seat, explained what he must try.

Out of the hatch and into the twilight. The ground heaved, more turtles were stirring about the immobile ones he had already shot. Blake used the torch. Beads of eyes glistened in its light, a vast pair of jaws snapped at his leg. The tough fabric of his suit tore. The jaws, even if they lacked teeth, closed with crushing force on his skin. Blake shot and saw his dart wink back and forth in the skin of a yellow lip. He staggered; the pain in his leg was a red agony shooting up to the hip. He wondered if the bone had been broken, crunched.

Somehow he got back into the hatch, pulled the door shut, half crawled into the cabin.

"Blake! The signal—help is coming!"

He levered himself up, caught the back of the seat, and with its aid got to his feet.

"Put on the cabin light," he gritted out.

When that flashed on, he blinked and then lurched to the control board. Press that button . . . pull this lever . . . turn up the com . . .

"X4-67 calling X4-39. Do you hear? Do you hear?" The voice was metallic. It might have issued from a machine, not a human throat, but the impulses which had launched it had.

Blake tried to shake off the fog spreading over him from the pain in his leg. Somehow he croaked back.

"X4-39—we hear. Unlisted level . . . unlisted level . . . damage . . . can not transfer . . ."

"X4-39—contact well established. Set full call-beam. Will ride that in."

"Difficult landing." Blake strove to marshal the warnings in order. "Have slid down hill. Also native race attack. Watch out for turtles—"

"Turtles!" He heard the incredulous note in that before he snapped the beam into continuous beacon call.

"Blake!" Marfy was on her knees, drawing the torn stuff of his suit and coveralls away from his leg. "You are hurt!"

He saw the raw flesh she bared. Whoever thought teeth were needed for biting?

"Our friends out there do not care to be put to sleep. I guess." He tried to use words to cover the pain he felt at her lightest touch. "Anyway, now the worst is over."

Or was it just beginning? demanded one unsuppressible thought through the waves of pain.

VI

BLAKE HAD BEEN right in his suspicion that worse was to follow their return from being lost on an uncoded world. His thoughts were gloomy as he lay on the narrow bed, his left leg in a mound of dressings. The usual starkness of the wardsmen's infirmary was an echo to his forebodings. Certainly the reception he had received—what he could remember of it—upon their return to Vroom had not been promising. He had always known that excuses were not popular in the corps, and now he lay adding up all the counts that might be filed against him.

Carrying of an unauthorized passenger probably headed the list. They had been lucky, so very lucky that they had been located in the turtle world. Otherwise, danger to Marfy Rogan rested directly on him. It did not matter to regulations that the rod failure prevented any request for passenger clearance, that his shuttle had been sabotaged. The prudent wardsman would have refused to give her seatroom, even on what should have been a safe return trip. Add to that the facts that he had not checked the shuttle thoroughly when carrying a passenger and that he had made contact adversely with natives on a hitherto unexplored level. Yes, those were all prime offenses and Blake would be very lucky to remain in the corps if charges were pressed on all of them!

There was a perfunctory rap at the door and Com Varlt entered, a tape recorder in one hand. His odd yellow eyes were bleak, his expression remote as he settled himself on the one chair the cell-like room provided and placed the machine, ready to go to work, on the small table at the head of Blake's bed.

"Report." The single word was an order as the senior's forefinger triggered the machine into action.

Blake wet his lips and began in the officially prescribed manner a report which was not in the least routine even if it was couched in the style he had been taught.

"Routine report—"

Varlt made an adjustment. "Classified report," he corrected sharply.

Blake digested that. So this was . . .

"Classified report," he amended. "Routine run to Project 6471. Agent: Blake Walker, Apt-wardsman, 7105, Shuttle, X4-39, under orders to . . ."

He went at it slowly, recalling each detail that might have some meaning for those by whom this report would eventually be studied. As he spoke, he could, he discovered, remember most details vividly. But it was a long task. Twice Varlt switched off while Blake took the medication which appeared in the table groove, but the senior wardsman asked no questions as Blake added fact to fact.

He came to the end with the final scene in the shuttle's cabin when, a little lightheaded with pain, he had waited with Marfy for the arrival of their crosstime rescuers, and now said the last formal words: "Attested by oath: Blake Walker, Apt-wardsman, 7105."

Varlt pressed the seal button, locking the recorder until its tape might be placed in the one and only reader entitled to broadcast it. His expression had not changed; he still wore that brooding, closed-in look.

"You accepted an unauthorized passenger." His words were clipped, impatient.

"I did."

"You made contact with other-level intelligent life, subjecting them to attack?"

"I did."

"Two counts will be so charged against your conduct record." The intonation of that was formal. But still Varlt did not rise to leave.

"You offer no defense?"

Blake would have shrugged, but lying upon one's back and being bound down by bandaging makes such a gesture close to impossible.

"No excuses, sir." He gave the approved answer.

"The techs have discovered extensive sabotage in X4-39 skillfully accomplished. This shall be taken into consideration when reviewing your case." And then that aloof surface cracked and Com Varlt came alive.

"This report—" he tapped the recorder—"is full, very full, and it is all fact. Now give me surmise, not just the facts."

Blake tried to raise his head and Varlt leaned forward to adjust a back rest for him.

"Either a Limiter plot, or the actions of an outlaw level-hopper."

"And the sabotage? Or do you suggest there is a tie between the Project and a hopper?"

"More probably Limiter. But why a Project tie with that, either? If a close-down is ordered, what would happen to them?"

"Yes. That presents us with a first-rate puzzle.

Any motive that fits one portion does not another. This much is the fact upon which we must build: Marva Rogan has vanished, and the X4-39 was never intended to reach Vroom. Do you realize how very lucky you were that you were found? Chance only dictated that, my young friend, the thinnest rim of chance!"

"I know. I wonder why the call system wasn't sabotaged, too."

"There was a try to do just that. Marks on the protecting encasing showed up when the techs made their examination. But either there was not enough time, which I am inclined to believe, or not the proper tools to wrench open the inner panel. This much we do know: there is someone at the Project who made every possible effort to insure your nonreturn? And why? Because you had Marfy on board? Or simply to insure that the Project would be cut off from communication with Vroom for a space? Or both together? Perhaps we may find out when the techs start work on the rods."

"The rods?"

Varlt nodded. "Yes. Why their failure also? We have checked the installation diagrams. There was no reason for their collapse, none possible—"

"Unless they were deliberately planted wrong," Blake said wearily.

His leg ached dully and there was a heavy weight pressing above and behind his eyes which was not quite pain, yet one which gnawed at him. All at once it did not matter to him, Blake Walker, as to what had happened hours ago on another successor world or what would happen here. He closed his eyes and then opened them with an effort, to see Varlt watching him.

The master wardsman rose and picked up the recorder. "What you need," he observed, "is sleep and not a puzzle to solve. See you forget all this for awhile."

Blake settled back. The heaviness in his head had progressed to pain. He swallowed a tablet the medic had left. As the dose dissolved on his tongue, he closed his eyes again, determined not to see, behind those lids, a rocky overhang hiding a betraying scratch in its shadow, scarlet lizards aiming spears, or a platoon of turtles bearing away the shuttle. And sleep engulfed him so that he did not.

For much of the next two days Blake continued to drowse, slipping in and out of sleep or a kind of bemusement which held little need for constructive thinking. But on the third morning he roused, clear-headed and restless. The medic assured him he was well on the mend and must exercise his leg. So he used crutches to reach a lounge and dropped into a chair there to see, outside a wide sweep of window, one of those fantastic gardens peculiar to this time level. With all crosstime to choose from, Vroom was a mixture of strange architecture, vegetation, ornaments, a place of magic for the eye, the ear, the nose. Plants, buildings, statues—the cities of Vroom were made up from samples taken from all the successor worlds known to their inhabitants. The garden before Blake was no exception.

He saw tree ferns, not unlike those of the turtle world, forming a backdrop to a fountain image of a winged man pouring water from a horn, while about the border of the octagonal pool were roses and scented flowers Blake could not name. Not too far away, a summer pleasure house seemed to be fashioned of lace frozen into crystal walls.

Vroom lived on crosstime. If the Limiters had their way, this life would be seriously curtailed. So much of Vroom's level had been blasted in the ancient atomic disaster that the habitable part was merely a string of oases. What moved the Limiters? What did they have to offer in place of the steady stream of supplies and trade that came via the shuttles to their home world? Strict control of such contacts was already in force; to shut down nine-tenths of those contacts as the Limiters wished would be to strangle Vroom.

"Blake!"

Shaken out of his thoughts, he looked over his shoulder.

Marfy Rogan, no longer wearing the drab coverall of the Project but in shimmering silk, with head veil, face stencils, other fashionable accessories of her set, came toward him. Behind her was a tall man whose very fair hair, green-blue eyes, and cast of countenance was the masculine duplicate of her own features and coloring.

He wore the short cloak of ceremony flung carelessly back, but Blake did not need to see the Hundred badge on the shoulder. He reached for his crutches to get to his feet, but Marfy whipped them away.

"Keep still," she ordered, and the touch of arrogance he had noted at their first meeting was back full force in her voice. "Father, this is Blake Walker."

Erc Rogan gave him the conventional greeting, hands out, palms down, wrists crossed, and then drew up two chairs, one for his daughter.

There was no one in the corps who had not seen

Rogan at one time or another, sometimes in inti-
mate comradeship during an expedition, or
merely as the official who was liaison between the
wardsmen and the Hundred. His nervous movements, his self-interrupted sentences, his air of
being only momentarily present between bouts of
furious action elsewhere, were familiar.

Now he did not settle into the seat he had chosen, but rather perched on its edge as if he could
be present for seconds only. And when he spoke,
it was with sharp, impatient abruptness.

"I have a full account of your adventure . . ."

The pause was only momentary. Blake made no
answer because he did not see that one was
needed. Erc Rogan was already speeding on.

"Marfy has told me her side of it."

Side of it? wondered Blake. That almost hinted
at some difference between their stories. He
glanced at the girl. In contrast to her father, she
appeared utterly relaxed, at ease. There was a
shadow of smile on her lips as if she found this
faintly amusing.

"I am satisfied with your part in the affair,
Walker." Rogan pulled at the edge of his official
cape as if he would like to rid himself of it altogether. "Therefore, I have requested you to be
assigned to this. They tell me you lack full psi.
Complete talents are not necessary in a team man.
If you are willing to take this one—"

"Erc Rogan!" Marfy said in a clear tone. "You
have not yet explained, none of it!"

For a second a frown showed between her
father's brows. Then he smiled.

"As usual I run before I walk, young man. Very
well, I shall explain. You have talked with Com;

you know the puzzle to be solved. My daughter is missing. I believe that she is level-hopping. She may have been tempted into beginning that willingly, but that cannot be the case now. Too long a time has elapsed. I do not know why. There can be more than one answer and each logical. But it is very"—he hesitated and then used a word which would have been understated and colorless save for the tone in which it was spoken—"necessary to find her. And it would seem that to do that we are faced with the dilemma of a man who drops a grain of sand into a measure of the same and then requires that original mote to be brought into view again. We have some thousand or more successor worlds on which we have contact, from regularly staffed depots to occasional visiting. We may be sure that Marva has not passed through any legal station. In all of this, there is only one clue and that is as unsubstantial as a spider's thread. Marfy knows that her sister has been fascinated by E625. There is a chance, so frail that I dare not rest any fraction of hope upon it, that she was taken there, ostensibly on a flying visit—"

"But they, whoever they are," put in Blake, "could have suggested such a goal and really stopped anywhere."

"Perfectly true." Erc Rogan gave a hard jerk and his cape loosened, slid down his arm. "But, it is all we have. And so we must follow it."

"The Project—what about whoever sabotaged the shuttle?"

"There is a ward team there now, sifting evidence. But if Marva is in the hands of an illegal hopper—I do not know why I pin any hope to this but I do—we must try it. If Marva is in E625, Marfy will know it. And once that fact is established either one way or another, we shall be ready to move on to the next step."

"Marfy?" Blake looked again to the girl.

This time she inclined her head. "I shall know if Marva is there. Therefore I am necessarily one of the party, Blake Walker. Despite all the rules, this is one time they will be broken."

"And this is a matter not to be discussed," Rogan interrupted his daughter. "Marfy is indispensable. We cannot search an entire world on any level, but she can let us know in a matter of hours of her sister's presence. Thus, we do break one of the first rules and allow her to accompany the search team. I shall be called to account for this and I am ready to answer—after you have gone. I do not risk my daughters for a matter of regulations. Marfy has lived with wardsmen's reports and accounts all her life and she has made all the crosstime trips allowed one of her sex. She is far from being ignorant of procedure. Only, until she has gone there will be no mention of this to anyone!"

"I promise." Blake felt that he was being pressured into this, but refusal to join the team was far from his mind. Rogan must know of the charges now on Blake's record. To make another trip might change the verdict concerning his future career, always supposing it was a successful one.

Rogan was out of his chair, dragging his cloak along the floor.

"Marfy," he was on his way to the door, "I have ordered the preliminary briefing tapes. You share them with Walker. The medic tells me you will be able to leave in three days, Walker. It will take perhaps six to finish indoctrination. But with a beginning—"

Marfy waved her hand. "Already we are beginning, Father. You need not worry about that."

Blake was not sure Rogan even heard that assurance. He had disappeared through the door before the last words were out of her mouth.

"So you get what you want!" Blake was not quite sure of his own reaction: irritation, a small wonder at her imperturbability, a suspicion that she might be finding this an exciting adventure without being much concerned at the cause.

"So I get what I want?" She made a question of the repetition. "Not to be a telepath, Blake Walker, must at times make one go as crooked and limping of mind as you now do of body. You require explanations where others need no words. But then, you are as a solid wall to me, and I must also depend on your words and guess from them and the tones of your voice what you think and feel. Now I believe you do truly wonder if Marfy Rogan is looking upon this as an adventure more than a plan to rescue Marva?"

Blake flushed. He might be mind-blocked as far as she was concerned, but still she read him as if he lay open to her lightest probe.

"You do not know us—Marva and me—therefore I do not find my anger greater than I can lay rein upon." Her voice was cool, a faint hint of amusement about her lips. "But without Marva, I go limping in my own way. It is not in me to wail, to act madly, without purpose. Perhaps in those first hours when I could not reach her, then fear was a poison in me, a taste in my mouth. But unless fear is built up by the imagination, as long as it remains steady, then it can be lived with, even used as a spur to action.

"Were I to remain here, unable to indulge in that action, then would I indeed know the whip of fear. And perhaps under it, I might break. But now I can do what I can to save Marva, and to that I bend my energy. I do not think that you or any of the team we join will find that I shall be the weak point. Now, shall we begin?"

From her belt bag, Marfy produced a hand-size recorder, a small and costly toy, which Blake recognized as one of the best obtainable. She moved her chair closer to his and set the machine on her knee, uncoiling from under the lid, two lines with small earphones. One she passed to him, the other she set under a loop of her elaborate headdress. When Blake nodded, she touched the lever and the tape began to spin its message for their hearing.

Later would come the viewer's pictures, the solid and detailed indoctrination, most of it taught under hypnosis. Now they merely skimmed the surface knowledge of a successor world.

Earlier in time E625 had been one with the world Blake had once called home. Then two crucial alterations of events had given it another future altogether.

The first came in 1485. Thereafter no Henry Tudor had reigned in England. Instead Richard the Third's courageous charge at his enemy during the Battle of Bosworth had carried him to the Lancastrian Pretender and, with his own hand, Richard had put an end to the Red Rose for all time.

Once firmly on the throne, Richard had developed the potentials that historians in Blake's world had come to grant him, with regret that he had never, in their own past, had a chance to show his worth as probably one of the ablest of the Plantagenet House. A marriage with a Scottish princess two years after Bosworth had provided him with both an heir and a peaceful border. And the Plantagenets had ruled England for another one hundred and fifty years. The brilliance that, in Blake's world, had marked the reign of Elizabeth Tudor, had in E625 flourished a generation earlier under Richard and his immediate successors.

Always mindful of the importance of trade, Richard had supported the Bristol merchants who sought new markets. One of the trading expeditions bound for Iceland sent two ships on into the unknown west of which the Norse had rumors, and the first fur trading station was planted on the American continent in 1505.

The second break that changed history as Blake had known it on his own level came on July 7, 1520. Cortes, driven out of Mexico City by the aroused Aztecs, fought a final battle near the village of Otumba. But this time an arrow struck down the determined and stubborn Spanish leader, and his demoralized men, already decimated during the retreat of the Noche Triste, had then, for the main part, ended their lives on the bloody altars of strange gods, leaving Quauhtemoc ruler in the land.

English traders with the Indians on the northern continent were followed by English fishermen plundering the finned wealth off shore; later, colonists spread down the Atlantic coast to form eventually the Nation of New Britain, now under only nominal control by the mother country.

Spain, lacking the gold of Mexico and Peru, had held on to a few of the West Indies until her king, deeply enmeshed in continental struggles for power, refused to send more support to his overseas subjects, and the Spanish Empire in the new world was a withered dream, over before it began.

Having, in E625, defeated the Spanish invaders, the Aztecs were confronted by troubles at home. The excessive bloodthirstiness of a religion that demanded endless sacrifices to their gods led to alliances between conquered peoples against them. And they, too, went down to defeat in a series of intertribal struggles. Some of the survivors fled northward to the southwest of what was now never to become, on this level, the United States. Spanish from the islands, adventruers from overseas, and neighboring New Britain, fished in these roiled waters and added their support first to one party and then the other.

But, by 1560, there was a sharp change in this uneasy situation. One of those leaders who sometimes rise in times of national turmoil came to the fore in Central America, reviving the ancient legends of the "white god." His antecedents were never known, but he stamped his rule so tightly on that region that his two sons and their descendants unified a collection of provinces into an empire such as the Aztec lords had never known. Under them, Mayan traders spread north, refugee colonies in the southwest were brought under control, and the territory west of the Mississippi slowly became a part of the new Empire.

New Britain and the Empire clashed in two wars, both indecisive. There had now been a period of peace, or armed neutrality, lasting about fifty years. Since then, the Empire had had frontier troubles in the north and difficulties with Russian colonists in the west. The Mississippi River made a natural boundary between two nations and two very different cultures. . . .

Merely a quick picture. There would be a great deal more to assimilate, Blake knew, before he would see that level for himself.

VII

"WILLIAM CAMPDEN, born in New Sussex at the
Manor of Gildenthorp, apprenticed to Giles
Goforth, accredited western merchant at the Port
of Ackrone. My father is a landowner in the honor
of Bradbury, and I am his third son. My brother
Rufus is a Commander in the Britannic Navy; my
brother Cadwalder is a merchant venturer in
China; my brother Richard is the heir and acts as
my father's bailiff . . ."

Blake did not have to mutter that aloud as he
reeled it out of a memory which at the moment
seemed overstuffed with strange lore, as if one
personality had been introduced willy-nilly to
cover the Blake Walker that was, leaving him with
a queer feeling of being two persons at once and
no longer well acquainted with either.

All the top-priority emergency processes of
Headquarters had been brought to bear to turn
him into this composite. Though Blake did not
accept hypnosis easily, they had worked patiently
and unceasingly on him, until he succumbed to
allow them to plant "William Campden" and William's past well enough to pass Vroom's rigorous
standards. And with William's background and
history had come all the material proper to place
Blake in a society that would accept him without
question.

"You have this much in your favor," Varlt had
said, "this cold war between the Toltec Empire
and New Britain does not make for free circula-
tion of the citizens of either in the enemy's terri-

tory. Of old, the Aztecs used their merchants as agent provocateurs, sending them into new country as forerunners of conquest, with definite orders to stir up trouble so that the military would have an excuse to take a hand. In fact, the whole social standing of the *pochteca*, the merchants, was based on the fact that they claimed to be soldiers in disguise. On the other hand, the way of life in the Mayan states was trade and not war, and their aristocracy was the merchants, making them highly jealous of their trade rights between one city state and the next. After the wars of uniting, Kukulcán the Second fostered the merchant class among both peoples. Such a move cut down the power of the military lords where he might reasonably find rebels and also gradually undermined the priesthood, which had already been discredited by the series of 'miracles' Kukulcán used to take over power at the beginning of his reign.

"During the last struggle between the two powers, New Britain had the edge to the extent that she forced through a commercial treaty with Toltec. Since then there has been a race to build up strength on both sides of the border, yet communication between them continues. Toltec has its troubles, with the frontier peoples to the north, and with the Russians in California. During the long minority of the present Emperor, Mayatzin, there has been a continuing and growing dispute between the merchants and the remnants of the old military nobility which can regain power only in times of war. There have also been rumors that the worship of Huitzilopochtli, the old Aztec god, has been secretly revived. Thus we walk a narrow ledge and we must be surefooted."

Now the team was about to plunge into E625, with only the slightest hope that what they sought there might be found. Blake looked at what lay on the table before him. The delicate beauty of that display would hold any man's attention. Even in his own world, before Charles of Spain's need for a war chest had ordered them into a common melting pot, men had marveled at the gold ornaments of Mexico. Here was the lineal descendant of that work, the original designs refined, altered, clarified, in a necklace and earrings found in Marva Rogan's jewel box in a secret compartment.

Not even Marfy had seen them before her search among her sister's possessions, for a clue had brought them into the open. Both had been identified unhesitatingly as Toltec. While Erc Rogan was sifting with care all the contacts his daughter had made during the past few months, striving to find some common denominator between E625 and his household, Marfy had become more silent and withdrawn. This proof that her tie with her sister had not been as complete as she had always believed it, seemingly cut deep.

From the sterile rock gorges of the Project world had come a chilling report. The wreckage of the lost 'copter had been found, caught in the toils of river rapids. That this meant the end of their search was accepted, on the surface, by Rogan and his daughter. But they did not believe that Marva, at least, had perished there.

Blake gave an impatient tug to the front of his new coat. The citizens of New Britain had never lost their taste for color as had the men of his own world when they accepted the drab uniformity of the late Victorian era. He now wore tight trousers of a dark, rich green, a ruffled and embroidered shirt of mulberry topped by a loose, widesleeved coat collared in narrow strips of fur and fastened, when he wished, with a gold clasp at the throat.

As exotic as their clothes might be, the New British were hardy, practical men of business. And they were "modern" in their industries as well. Transportation was largely via electrically powered vehicles. Horsedrawn carriages remained, however, as status symbols. Air travel was limited to short distances via low flying "wings," mainly for military purposes. An invention some twenty years back had closed the borders of both nations to air crossing by setting up sonics no wing could penetrate.

As a merchant, William Campden carried no side-arms, though his brothers in their various activities would all be equipped with ceremonial swords, shorter than the weapon Blake knew by that name. So the broad belt about his waist had on it only the buckle which bore the arms of his family, and so established his rank. An intensive course in identifying heraldic buckles had been a part of his study lest he make some slip in paying deference where it was due.

"Walker?" Varlt, wearing clothes similar to Blake's save that he had chosen blue and yellow, his fur collar was wider, his embroidery more ornate, his belt supported the "sword" of a master merchant, and his buckle proclaimed his alliance with a noble house, stood in the door. "We are ready."

In a way the new team was a reunion of old comrades-in-arms. Pague Lo Sige, whom Blake had once known as Stan Erskine, another of the man-hunting group which had prowled successor worlds, was one of them. His slight fairness was more pale; he seemed fragile in the bulky overcloak of a merchant.

Marfy stood a little apart. While her skirt was short, barely sweeping her knees, her legs were discreetly covered with tights of black, lavishly patterned in silver-thread designs. The dress itself was a straight sheath of silver gray, bearing no ornamentation at all save the shield on her belt. Over this she wore a slightly longer sleeveless coat of a darker shade of gray. The whole effect was one of mononotone to the knees, bright decoration below. Her hair had been sacrificed to her disguise, cropped almost as short as a man's, with the tips of separate locks dyed red-brown, giving her head a curious dappled appearance, the height of fashion in New Britain.

Erc Rogan was with her, his hand clasping her forearm as if, in these last minutes, he nursed a second thought about the risk of her journey. But, though he walked so, hand upon her, he offered no protest as the team entered the shuttle cabin.

Vroom had a depot on E625—there was no "chance" in this trip—and the shuttle had been minutely examined before they took off. Yet Blake could not help tensing as the familiar dizziness gripped him. Unconsciously he awaited some disaster. Then he realized his fear and was angry. Was he going to have always a suspicion concerning time transfer?

There was no conversation in the cabin. Perhaps, like Blake, the others, too, spent the period of travel reviewing points of indoctrination, striving to make sure of their new identities of William Campden, Geoffrey Warnsted, his niece Ann Warnsted, and Matthew Lightfoot.

The warning arrival signal settled them more deeply into their seats as the spin-through began. Then they came out into a screened-off section of a warehouse. Headquarters had calculated their entrance to occur under the cover of night and only the faintest of lights guided them down a narrow aisle between crates and bales. The gleam that beckoned them was in place over a door. Varlt motioned them to a halt and opened the portal cautiously.

Outside was a walled yard paved with stone blocks, and awaiting them was a vehicle, a truck for transporting goods. Varlt and Blake took their seats in front, Marfy and Lo Sige in the curtained van. As if he carried a map in his head and had been driving such a van most of his life, Varlt started the motor, swung the car through the yard gate and then through a maze of streets, all lighted with rods set up pillar-fashion at measured intervals. The buildings about them were of stone or concrete for the first four or five stories, towering beyond that point in more floors which appeared to be made of wood. There were no advertising signs, but fanciful, ornamental lanterns marked some of the structures in blazes of color, identifying the nature of the business housed within.

"Here." Varlt brought the truck under an archway into another court as poorly illuminated as the one that had flanked the warehouse. Together they entered the building. During their swift passage through the streets, they had seen only a scattering of people and those, men. This city on the frontier had curfew laws in strict enforcement, and few women lived here permanently.

The man waiting for them inside was stout of body, his coat that of a master merchant. A pointed beard of iron gray added to his general air of unquestioned authority. Roger Arshalm, English merchant out of London, was neither "English merchant" nor "out of London," but he was accepted by all of Port Ackrone as just that.

With a few words of what seemed to Blake grudged recognition, certainly not of greeting, he hurried them up a stairway to the wood-walled upper floors, the section which, for every merchant, provided living quarters for him, his family and all of his resident staff.

Within a well-lighted, paneled room, Arshalm flung off his outer coat and waved them to a table where wine pooled in beautifully fashioned cups and there were metal plates rimmed in enameled jeweled colors, each filled with fruits, wafers, or rounds of bread spread with paste mixtures which Blake could not identify but which smelled appetizing.

"This is madness," Arshalm was blunt. "You, lady," he looked at Marfy, "are a risk here. There are so few women in town that each and every one is known, with her history reaching back three generations. To have you sighted will stir up such comment as might break cover for all of us at the depot. You," now he turned to the rest of the company, "I can make shift to account for. There is unease along the river. You can be ordered out of the Empire on some lord's whim, forced to leave with only what you have on your backs—"

"That sort of thing is happening?" Varlt cut in. "Trouble brewing?"

"It is happening, yes. Trouble has always been

brewing here, but to my mind it is now coming to a seething boil!"

"Any special reason?"

Arshalm threw up his hands. "Reason? The old one of the merchants wanting peace, the lords, seeing their power and their holdings dwindling, war. With rumors of wild practices along the frontiers and in less isolated spots, too. Then, the prophecy of Huitzilopochtli's return is being mouthed. A long minority for a ruler never makes for a stable kingdom; there is more than one lord who begins to see himself wearing the Imperial green."

"But all of this has been going on for years—"

"And building up to a nasty situation through all of them. The time grows short and the lords are beginning to show such boldness as they have not displayed since the abortive uprising back in 1912. They are hauling out forgotten laws, putting them into use when and where they can. The latest is containment for foreign Allowed Merchants. They are 'allowed' out of their houses only by pass and under guard—for their own good, of course. The populace resents foreigners—that is the given reason with a few controlled riots to give it credence. Some carefully manufactured incidents and they will have an excuse for expelling all the Allowed—"

"And New Britain's stand on that?"

"With the present government?" Arshalm shrugged. "No move in the immediate future. But if there is a ground swell of public opinion, the Moderates may be thrown out of power and the Kingsrule party will be in. The Viceroy is walking a very narrow path to keep the peace. And he can only advise, he can not order. The Diversification of 1810 is complete as to the legality of home rule."

"So, unless you find what you seek in New Britain—" Arshalm was continuing when Marfy made a sudden, uncontrolled gesture, sending the goblet before her crashing over to flood the cloth with wine.

She did not even glance down at those spreading yellow ripples. Instead her head turned, not as if she willed it but as if flesh and bone were drawn about, steel to magnet.

With her head still held to that angle, she rose from her chair, leaving them staring after her. Now she turned slowly to face completely around, walking, her eyes wide, moving to a tapestry hanging along the wall. Her hands fumbled with its folds, parted them, to uncurtain a window. The girls fingers now rose to the fastening of the casement, plucked at its latch.

Varlt moved first, covering the distance between them in a couple of wide strides, pushing aside her hands to open the casement for her. Night air swept in, cool, and with it the sound of water. Flecks of light marked the lanterns. Varlt's hands fell gently on Marfy's shoulders in a gesture that combined support and protection.

"Marfy." His voice was low, coaxing.

She swayed under his touch, but her head did not turn; she still stared out into the night. Then Blake saw the shudder that ran through her whole body, as if she had been plunged into icy water to awake roughly into the here and now. She turned under Varlt's hold and clung to the front of his loose coat; her features were worn and strained.

"I was right." Her voice was thin, low, but so still were the rest in that room that it carried easily. "Marva is here!"

"Can you find out where?" Varlt's voice was as gentle as his grasp. "Where is Xomatl?" she asked in turn.

Arshalm made a move as uncontrolled as the one that had upset Marfy's goblet. Varlt looked at the depot officer over Marfy's head.

"It is in Empire territory, south, one of the tribute centers. If she is there in truth . . ." He shook his head.

"New Britain has no contacts there at all?" Varlt demanded.

"There is a supervised caravan of Allowed Merchants escorted there every second month, or has been in the past. What will continue to be done is any man's guess. But the credentials of such merchants, they are impossible to obtain. The same families have had that trade for generations. It would be impossible to plant anyone in such an expedition, even if there is another."

Varlt looked back at Marfy. "Are you sure?"

"Yes. She—she is kept close but they do not call her prisoner. If I can try with a full-mind probe, maybe . . ."

This time Varlt's nod was brisk. "That you shall do. Arshalm, you have the necessary privacy? Marfy, will you need a booster drug?"

"Let me try unaided first. We have never used the drug and have always done well in the past."

With Arshalm and Varlt, she left the room. Blake knew something of the ordeal facing her though he had never undergone it himself. Mind-to-mind communication on the highest level induced in the participants a condition akin to trance. They must be allowed privacy and a state of complete silence and rest. This would be given Marfy here, but would her twin have the same untroubled state from which to answer? A thousand to one chance had paid off. Marfy's guess as to her sister's whereabouts had been proven true. But where did they move now—and how?

Lo Sige finished the last of his wine. Now he smiled at Blake and shrugged as if he could read the younger man's mind.

"Guessing at our next move? Do not waste the mental energy. We will take no action until we are sure. Arshalm cries 'impossible' now, but he is already striving to pick holes in his own verdict. We have but to preserve our patience for a space. What lies immediately before you and me is bed".

And when Blake was lying in the fourposter bed with its curtains and fine, lavender-scented linen clean and cool about his body, he did relax after a fashion. There was the patina of age in this room, the feeling that time in some respects had passed less swiftly, and that some of the trappings of another, more stately, age had lingered on to provide a feeling of security and identification with one's forefathers which was missing in his home world.

He had flung open his casement before going to bed, and the sound of the river was a murmur in the room. One thing about Port Ackrone—there was no roar of traffic lasting through the night.

The river, and beyond it, the enemy territory. Somewhere, to the southwest, another city even more alien than this, and in it, for a purpose they could not yet fathom, Marva. When did the improbable truly ever become the impossible? They were here on the same level as Marva, when that chance had been so small as to be incredible. Would luck continue to ride with them?

The murmur of the river was soothing and Blake drifted between half sleep and waking. Then he awoke. Far off for now, a mere shadow of a shadow of a shadow, peril stalked. His talent offered him only slight irritation as yet, but it was awake. Not the natural unease to be expected under the circumstances, but a definite warning of danger lying in wait. However, it was still not a loud call to arms, just that shadow of a shadow of a shadow. Reaching from the southwest?

VIII

"MADNESS!" Arshalm had come up from the shop rooms below. As he strode back and forth, the skirts of his coat flapped agitatedly, giving him the semblance of a bird of ill omen about to soar. "The news has just come through, they are expelling merchants from Tonoçahl and Manao."

"But still the caravan is prepared to move to Xomatl, is it not?" Varlt sat hunch-shouldered at the table, staring at a map weighted open by various pieces of tableware. "These towns you mention are both in the north. Any reason why the Toltecans should do this now?"

"They are both in the old frontier lands," Arshalm answered rather absentmindedly.

"Merchants have always been suspect there," Lo Sige commented. "The plains warriors—they were only beaten into submission about two generations ago. It was their uprising against the Empire that really turned the tide in the last war and saved western New Britain from being overrun. They have never taken kindly to Empire rule, and they could well provide a weapon for intrigue, just ready to be aimed."

Arshalm paused by the table. "That is entirely true. And the signs are all of a volcano about to erupt. If any British are across the border when it happens, Heaven help them! Nothing on *this* earth will! The fanatics shall want a blood feast following the old customs, and it was always the rule that you first used a stranger's blood to feed the gods."

"Marva is there." Into the silence which had followed the merchant's outburst, Marfy's three words fell, oddly shrill. There were shadows under her eyes; she might have risen from a serious illness.

"But more than just that you do not know," Arshalm returned abruptly.

"I was not . . . able . . . to learn more. Why I do not know."

Marfy's struggle to communicate via mind probe had brought her no closer contact with her sister. And that disturbed them all, delivering a shock from which Marfy had not yet recovered.

"Mind block?" Lo Sige glanced from the girl to Varlt and then on to Arshalm.

"Possible," Varlt replied first.

"No one on this level is capable of that," Arshalm denied.

"Never underrate a native priesthood," remarked Lo Sige, and then added, "She did not reach this world unescorted, and she was brought here for a definite purpose. To that we are all agreed. Those who brought her here must have taken precautions."

"We must find her! Marfy's voice held a hint of hysteria now. "What if . . . if she was brought as a . . . gift?"

Vroom consciences were not entirely clean in that direction. Too many Vroomian families had imported initially unwilling brides, kidnapped from other successor worlds, to found their clans. The Rogans probably had at least one of those in their past history, one whose story would be well known to her descendants. Marfy's guess was a logical one.

Varlt shook his head. "No, this is not a matter of wife-stealing. If that were the case, she would have been given false memories, not plunged directly into another level as a prisoner. What's more, such a gift would be unacceptable in Toltec. One of your type, Marfy, would have no interest for a member of the court or the nobility. Or . . ." He stopped abruptly; his mouth tightened into a grim line.

Marfy cried out, half rose from the table, her hands at her mouth in a gesture of horror, as if to prevent her own lips from uttering something too terrible to be said aloud. Not for the first time Blake longed for telepathic powers. Whatever idea had just flashed into Varlt's mind had sped in turn to the girl and, judging by his expression, also to Lo Sige, though Arshalm merely looked puzzled. Blake decided that the merchant's psi powers must lie in other directions.

"So"—Lo Sige's fingertips beat a tattoo on the board—"it would seem that speed is now matter of importance—"

He was interrupted as Varlt spoke to Arshalm. "That makes it imperative! We have to be on that caravan when it leaves two days from now. How can it be done?"

Arshalm pounded a fist on the table. "I have already said! It cannot be! Three British families have the hereditary trading rights in Xomatl: the Wellfords, the Frontnums, the Trelawnlys. Everyone they send is personally known to the guards, the frontier patrols, the merchants in Xomatl. No substitutions can be made; it would be known at once."

Lo Sige smiled lazily. "There is no insoluble

problem," he said with deceptive mildness. "Have you a complete list, plus viewer report, on every man who will go?"

Arshalm took a packet from one of the inner pockets of his coat and threw it on the table. "Six men, every one of them known as well to those over the river as they would be known to their own brothers."

Lo Sige opened the packet, fed the tape roll within to a small viewer and aimed the machine at the wall of the room. The picture was not as clear as it would be on a real screen, but bright enough for them to see each man as he appeared. Six men, ranging from middle age to youth, with the eldest being Master Merchant James Frontnum, the rest two assistants, an apprentice, and two general packers, the latter ambitious youngsters learning their trade.

"Every one of them either a Frontnum, a Wellford, or a Trelawnly, even the packers!" Arshalm declared. "We could not supply a single newcomer."

"Thus," Lo Sige said gently, "we make a clean sweep and supply a whole company."

Blake expected Arshalm to run true to form with instant protest. But the merchant did not reply with an outburst. Instead, he sat down and surveyed them all in turn.

"You know, this not merely reckless," he stated in a mild, conventional tone, "it is simply utter madness. Oh," he waved a hand as if to stall any replies, "we can turn you out as visual copies of these men. We can get you briefings of a sort. But none of that will hold up once you are across the river and among suspicious men who know the

Allowed Merchants with the intimacy of years, who also look upon all foreigners as potential spies. They know these men," he jerked a thumb at the tape and its burden of pictures, "probably better than they know themselves."

"Granted," Varlt agreed.

"Then you admit that it cannot be tried." Varlt frowned at the viewer. "It will have to be—if what I fear is so—it must be!"

Marfy still sat with her fingers pressed to her lips. Her eyes were very large and had some of the sheen Blake had seen in the eyes of terrified animals. He was still at a loss as to what they all feared, but he realized that it was serious enough to push Varlt past the edge of caution.

"And what is so important?" Arshalm asked almost plaintively.

"Old customs," Varlt replied with visible reluctance. "Very old customs. Think, man, why might one present a stranger—and a maiden—to certain parties over the river?"

Arshalm stopped the nervous smoothing of his coat where it lay across his knee. Under his gray brows his eyes sharpened in a gaze pinned on Varlt. Then his breath was expelled in a hiss.

"No!" His protest against his own thoughts was forceful, but against his will he now shared Varlt's forebodings.

And now Blake understood, too. A most grisly memory flashed into his mind, leaving in its wake a retching sickness so that he swallowed convulsively. There was a story out of the past, enough to turn any man's stomach.

The early-wandering Aztecs, seeking a homeland, had made a temporary alliance with a city

king in the fertile valley of their dreams. Together
successful in war, due to the superiority of the
Aztec warriors, the Aztecs had suggested a further
alliance by marriage, the king's daughter as wife
for their chief. And the king, considerably impressed by the vigor and military prowess of these
wild men out of the north, had agreed. But when
he and his court came to attend a feast in celebra-
tion of the marriage, they had seen a priest dance
before a savage and alien god, his robe of office the
flayed skin of the princess! When the outraged
king and his followers turned upon their late al-
lies and drove them back into the lean wilderness,
the Aztecs had not really understood, for in their
eyes they had done honor to both god and princess.

Yes, there was darkness and blood in the past.
And what if there was a return to those ways of
horror . . .

"But that was over six hundred years ago,"
Blake burst out. "No one could do that now!"

"Old beliefs die hard, and they can be revived to
serve the needs of desperate men. United in guilt
men may be more easily led. There have always
been smoldering brands of the old religion in the
Empire. They may have been forced to turn to
other ways, but the power of the priests has held
in some pockets. They exiled one of the greatest of
their early leaders, Quetzalcoatl, because he
would do away with blood sacrifice. When the
chaos of the civil war back in 1624 finally tossed
Kukulcán the Second into the rule and the priesthood was put down, there was a period of reli-
gious revival or awakening. But never were the
old gods totally destroyed. Oh, I know that the

leaders give no personal credence to Huitzil-opochtli, Xipé, or any other. But blood ceremonies have their place in uniting and exciting those they would lead. One great and relatively open ceremony might well send the whole Empire spinning into another uprising in which those who wish and will can fish for the power they are avidly seeking."

"You are right," Arshalm spoke heavily as if admitting it took some virtue out of him. "Also, the date . . ."

"Fifty-two year cycle—the ancient kindling of new fire."

Varlt glanced at Lo Sige and the chill in his look would have frozen Blake had the stare been turned on him. But the younger man only nodded at his superior as if acknowledging some silent order passed between them

Blake's briefing supplied him with the importance of Lo Sige's remark. The ancient Kingdoms of the Sun, all of them, had been rigidly rule by astronomy and their numerical systems based upon a fifty-two-year cycle. At the end of that span of years there was a colossal "New Year" period. All debts were canceled, hostilities ended, agreements and contracts terminated. Each housewife threw out all her pots and pans and her furniture, and prepared to replace them with new. And the new fire, marking the beginning era, had been kindled on the breast of a sacrificial victim.

"Ending of old, beginning of new," Marfy said. "Then it is the time for us to chance . . . Oh, Com!"

The master wardsman did not reach across the table to take her hand; he did not nod. But from him to the girl must have flowed some reassurance, for she relaxed visibly.

"Can you pick up all the members of the caravan?" he asked Arshalm brisky.

"Yes. I could offer them a banquet here. It is often common to entertain colleagues about to embark on trading trips, to try to persuade the venturers to take some of one's specialties along. Since I am English, they would believe in such a gesture on my part. But—we have only two days."

"Let us be thankful for that much!" was Varlt's reply.

Afternoon, dusk, dawn, then the first hour of a new day. Blake peered into a mirror. He was no longer Blake Walker nor William Campden; he was now Rufus Trelawnly. His merchant's coat and other badges of some small rank were missing, save for a heraldic belt buckle. Now he wore dark rust trousers, a dull green shirt, and over it a sleeveless, tight-fitting jerkin which left him more muscle freedom for the heavy labor demanded by his present station of packer.

Varlt was now James Frontnum; Lo Sige, Richard Wellford; and Marfy, Denys Frontnum. Two wardsmen had joined them, sharing Blake's rank of packer. They were volunteers from Headquarters, not from among Arshalm's staff, since the absence of those would be noted.

The native New British they were replacing had been—first, under mental control and then in drugged sleep—removed to Vroom. When they returned, they would be supplied with false memories to cover the period of their absence. Or that was the present hope.

"There it is." A short time later Blake looked along the wharf, following the pointing finger of the man who pushed a twin package-carrier to the one he himself trundled. The river boat, intended mainly for cargo, waited them. Her crew were darker-skinned subjects of the Empire and scarlet-bagged soldiers were visible along her deck. Most of the heavy cargo had been on board for days. Those carriers Blake and his companion were responsible for contained the cream of what the caravan had to offer, most of it exotic luxuries designed for the nobility, for the court, some of it for "gifts."

Could they carry off the imposture? Their briefing in their new roles had been so speedy that it had merely scraped the surface, and Blake was not sure how long they could go undetected among the ever-suspicious enemy.

"Step lively, you!" Varlt looked back with just the proper amount of irritation, waving the carriers ahead. So that Blake and his fellows were the first on deck.

In shape the vessel was a blunt-angled triangle, with the width at the stern. There was no visible means of propulsion; whatever power sent it waddling along was hidden. And the merchant party was not encouraged to explore.

Once on board all of them had been herded astern, a latticework of bars slammed shut and locked, leaving them to their own devices in what was an effective prison. They even furnished their own food supplies. Not only were they locked in, but there was an alert pair of sentries beyond the bars, changed every four hours. However, all this was according to usual practice.

"We are on our way," Lo Sige observed. "And what is our next move?"

"If all goes well," Varlt explained, "we disem-

bark, as always, at the Pier of the East in Xomatl.
But we are not lodged near there. They march us,
under guard all the way to the south of the city
where we stay in the Strangers' House—more like
a prison than a house! Then we set up the gifts for
the Port captain, the head of the local Merchants'
Guild, the resident *tonalpoulqui* who practices
divination and will give us a good day for trade.
All this is regular procedure. If the gifts are acceptable, we are told the trade day and the *Pochteca Flatoque* at the head of the Guild move in to
inspect. We may have three days, even more, between arrival and the beginning of trade. Perhaps
we can string it out even longer by lagging a little
on the gifts, but we dare not arouse suspicion—"

"They will watch us every minute!" cut in one
of the new team members.

"That they will," Varlt agreed.

As far as Blake could see, they did not have a
chance. Yet he had faith in Varlt and Varlt's experience. Somewhere, the master wardsman must
see a loophole, even if he were not yet so sure of it
as to explain.

Blake's own personal warning was no stronger,
just lay like a shadow within his mind, a momentary chill now and then along his spine. Having
helped stow the rest of the cargo so that all would
appear as usual to the guard, he finally went out
on the slice of deck that was allowed them. At this
point, the river was wide and they had swung
diagonally across it to coast along the Empire's
shore, with the flood now between them and New
Britain. From all Blake could see, the wilderness
they were slipping past might never have been
penetrated by men at all.

Twice before dusk, breaks showed small land-ings in that green wall. But neither time did the boat approach them, nor could Blake sight any signs of life about the clearings. He went into the cabin for the evening meal. All were present but Lo Sige.

A moment later he appeared to say crisply, "There is a Jaguar officer on board!"

"You are sure?" Varlt asked.

"He was up on the spy deck just now watching us. And there is no mistaking his badge. You know the custom; no one can wear that insignia save men granted it in full ceremony."

"A Jaguar officer . . ." Varlt chewed upon that.

The military élite of the old Aztec kingdom carried over into the Empire two companies of proven warriors: Jaguars and Eagles. The men in each of these groups attained their positions only after winning many battle honors. Even though the Empire had not been officially at war for a generation, a series of frontier struggles gave the ambitious the means of military advancement. Very few of the merchants, for all their power, even had had their sons chosen to wear the snarl-ing beast-mask badge or the eagle with out-stretched wings. Such distinction rested mainly with the old nobility.

"He might be on frontier inspection, taking this ship by chance, and curious—"

"I do not trust such coincidences," Varlt re-turned.

Marfy retired early to her cabin, but Varlt, Lo Sige, and the senior of the volunteers continued to sit about the table. There was an atmosphere suggesting that juniors had better keep their distance, and Blake went back on deck. The tramp of the sentries came in a regular thud-thud. Both were armed, not only with long belt knives but also this world's equivalent of a rifle, a weapon which shot a burning ray rather than a solid projectile.

Blake sought the rail on the landward side. Here, too, a net or grill rising some six feet or more above the deck made it clear that those inside were to stay there. Not that landing anywhere along that dark shore would avail a man. Any skulker would be hunted down by trained war hounds and equally savage men should he attempt to travel through what appeared to be a tangled wilderness.

"*Teyaualouanìme!*" The word came out of the shadows masking the upper deck, sounding almost like a snake hiss. Something plopped to the deck with a soft noise. Blake reached out a hand and caught at the half-seen object, to discover his fingers had closed on a rope ladder.

"Up!" ordered the voice from above. There had been a light there earlier, but now that whole section was dark. Blake could make out only a shadowy figure near the top of the ladder. "Up!" came the order again, this time more imperatively.

Someone had addressed him by the old name indicating a merchant spy in the service of the Empire and now had ordered him to climb out of what was legal confinement much as if he expected such a summons. If he refused, it might well be that he would endanger the disguise of the whole party. But who? And why?

Blake climbed up over the rail above to the deck

sacred to the officers of the guard and the vessel.

"The Day is nine. Who runs through the streets with a blackened face?" The words were in the English of New Britain but delivered with a hissing intonation. And Blake, totally unable to answer the gibberish which must have some meaning both to his accoster and the real Trelawnly, dared not answer.

"The Day is nine—" the other began again. Then Blake caught the sound of boot soles striking heavily against the decking.

At the same moment Blake's sense of danger was no longer only a lurking shadow; it flared into a demand for instant defense. He dodged back, away from the inner rail where the ladder still held. But the other, still only a shadow, sprang after, either in attack or an effort to get Blake undercover. The wardsman's hips met the side rail; he grabbed wildly for a hold. There was a rush. No—this other meant to aid! Blake's ankles were seized in a fierce grip and he was dumped over and down, into the swirl of the river below. . . .

IX

BLAKE SPRAWLED face down in sticky mud, the
smell of rotting vegetation chokingly strong, the
slime of a manytimes flooded reed bank smeared
on arms and body. He was not quite sure just how
he had reached this spit in the dark. Some instinct
of self-preservation had brought him through the
madness out on the river when rays had lashed
the water about his flailing arms as he had tried to
keep from drowning. They must have thought
that they had got him, or else they did not greatly
care, content to leave him to the shore patrols.

He roused enough to crawl on, farther out of the
tug of the river water, up into the crackling reed
bed. Then he ventured to sit up and try to sort out
the happenings on the boat. Clearly he had been
summoned to a secret meeting, greeted with a
password to which he had no key. Then someone
probably not in the secret had come along the
deck, and his half-seen companion had taken a
drastic means of getting rid of a possible betrayer
by dumping Blake overboard. That might not be
the reason for his present plight, but as an explanation it held together sensibly.

Now he was ashore, and in territory where he
was fair game for the first inhabitant who sighted
him. He had two choices: to try to recross the river
to New Britain, or to work his way downstream
and rejoin the merchant ship. And the way he felt
now, Blake was not too certain either was possible. For he had not come out of that barrage of rays

untouched. Between shoulder and elbow on his left arm a raw, seared strip some three fingers wide proved that, and to move his arm at all brought a wave of sickening pain. To swim with that hurt—here where the river was so wide and the current swift—no.

On the other hand, there was drift caught all along the shore. This river, in his own successor world, was notorious for its changes of course and its floods, and the same must be true here. If he could find drift to support him, he might take to the river again and win through, even reach the boat, where, of course, he might be shot on sight.

On the other hand he might be welcomed aboard by those who would like to hear about his meeting with the stranger on the upper deck. Blake was certain that the intrigant had been an army officer. And what possible connection would there be between one of them and the foreign merchants they considered their bane and long-declared enemies?

Blake rose unsteadily to his feet. He could not go on through the reed bed, his feet were sucked deeply into its muck as he tried to walk. Better get to higher ground. But this was a moonless night and Blake only located a high bit of land by blundering face on into a bank. Somehow he won to the top of that. He lay down and rolled over on his back, panting with the effort, his burned arm across his chest.

Small sparks of light danced under the dark curtains of bushes—fireflies. And as he lay still, Blake caught night sounds: the hoot of an owl, a splash as some animal took to the water, then—a barking which sent a shiver through him. Hound of some patrol?

To thresh about blindly in the dark was not sensible. But the longer he remained where he was, the farther away the boat would be, the greater the chance of being found by a patrol. Get to it. Get to it!

Blake stood up. The curve of the river bank here was southwest. There were trees and brush about him but not enough to worm a barrier. He went on at a pace which was closer to a stumble than a walk. Twice more he heard that distant barking. And once a black blot snorted and stampeded noisily through the bushes away from his path. He began to count: five hundred; then rest for a hundred; five, then rest. It was too dark to look for drift beneath the bluff, but as soon as the first gray of morning arrived he would go down to the water's edge and find what he needed.

New Britain kept patrol cruisers on her side of the river, Blake remembered now. Find his drift for support, get across the river, well away from this dangerous and inhospitable shore. He could claim, if picked up by the British authorities, to be one of the exiles from up-river, fleeing from the hostility of Imperial nobles. Blake was proud of that piece of planning. He was too warm and his arm, thrust into the front of his jerkin for support, ached with a throb which every stumble sent jabbing up into his shoulder and across his chest. So that sometimes it seemed he could not breathe as deeply as his exertions demanded, and he was forced to stand gasping for a wasted moment or two.

The night went on forever, as if time, as a measured thing, had ceased to exist and he was doomed for eternity to waver on through the dark, sometimes tripped by roots or ground-hugging branches. Blake moved in a stupor now. His personal danger signal had faded to a general alert, just as it had in the shuttle when he approached the Project. The shuttle—Varlt—Marfy—the boat. Dully the immediate past moved through his mind, but as if none of that action had concerned him in any way. What *was* important was the next step, and the next, and the next—if he could continue to take them.

Blake fell again, this time landing full upon his injured arm. And he could not stifle a sharp cry, just as he had no defense against a blackness thicker than the night. So he remained where he was as the sky began to pale overhead.

Rain awoke him, blowing in chill gusts under the branches to rewet his soaked clothes. Blake blinked stupidly as he opened his eyes and tried to understand where he was. Rain—branches—he was in the open. How? What? The big drops washing his face restored a portion of memory. He was on a successor world. The boat . . . the river . . . he had been following the river. And now it was day, he could easily distinguish the vegetation about him. Drift . . . the river bank . . . he had to get away!

He was pulling himself up by the aid of a bush when he was frozen by a low snarl—and the stab of his inner alert. Blake turned very slowly to face the source of the sound. Slitted eyes, glittering green, looked at him with a calculating hunter's interest, a promise of self-confident savagery. Ears flattened to a round, feline skull, as breath hissed in warning between sharp white fangs. Puma? No, this was a jaguar, one of the spotted jungle lords of the far south, out of its home territory but very much the master of the situation.

It advanced a paw, inched forward in a stalk, with belly fur brushing the ground as it came. Around its neck was a collar set in green gems. Again that warning snarl, and Blake calculated his chances. Behind him, surely not too far away, was the edge of the river bluff. Could he make it over that drop before the cat sprang? He doubted it.

The jaguar paused, raised its head. Now it voiced a yowl which was close to a scream, and was answered by another snarl from between Blake and the lip of the bluff. He was fairly caught! Watching the stalker before him as if he could hold the beast by his will, Blake backed a little so he could see in the other direction. His inner alert was steady, as if the cats were not yet to be considered deadly.

Another sleekly furred head moved into sight. This one was less easy to distinguish in the undergrowth for the fur was black, making the white of the bared fangs stand out sharply. The second beast did not advance into the open. Water dropped from it and it snarled, shaking its head vigorously. The spotted cat was now lying down, and it, too, snarled and hissed with the rain's wetting. Neither animal showed an inclination to attack, but that they were on guard against any attempt to move on his part, Blake did not doubt.

Hunting *cats!* He had been warned about the hounds of the river patrols, vicious, notorious for their tracking as well as their often fatal attacks upon fugitives. But these cats were different; they had not been covered in his briefing. Personal pets of some local lord? The jaguar was a sacred animal; the Emperor sat on a throne fashioned in the likeness of one, and they had given their name to the elite military caste.

Blake did not have long for speculation. His inner alert gave a new thrust. He glanced from one animal to another. Neither had moved, nor were they crouched to spring. But from some distance away came a dull booming, repeated thrice. The black cat disappeared as if sucked back into the heart of the bushes by the call. Now came other sounds like drumbeats. Danger . . . close . . . danger . . .

He moved, and his movement was met by a crescendo snarl. The spotted cat crouched, ready to spring. Blake stiffened. Not too far away there was a yowling feline scream answered by shouts. He was clearly trapped and the cats' masters were on their way to gather him in.

A mixed crew came up to his stand. The first of them wore tanned leather breeches and sleeveless loose shirts of cotton, dyed green and brown in mottled patterns, barely covering their muscular chests and shoulders. Their hair was drawn back and tightly clubbed at the napes of their necks, and they wore splashes of paint on their foreheads. Retainers of some lord, his hunter-rangers, all of them carried the blowpipes of hunters, not the more sophisticated side arms of the military, and each shirt also bore on the breast a crest badge.

The spotted cat rose from its crouch and paced a step or two away. None of the hunters spoke to it, but they made a path for its passing as if it were a high-born lord. It sat down on its haunches and raised a forepaw to lick.

Meanwhile, the leader of the party snapped his fingers and two of his men approached Blake, taking thongs from collections at their belts. His injured arm was twisted callously behind him and his wrists secured together in the workmanlike manner of those used to transporting game. A shove on his shoulder set him walking. So escorted by the whole party, plus the cat, he wavered on.

Blake stumbled so many times, that at last the leader, with a grunt of exasperation, told off one of the others to walk beside their prisoner and keep him steady. Even if he had been unbound and fully able, Blake knew he could never equal the woodsmanship of these men. They were Amerindians of the northern tribes, the plains rovers who some generations back had been incorporated into the Empire after a series of pitched battles and guerrilla warfare. Nowadays they were drawn upon for frontier and ranger duty. All were tall, well-made, akin to the Cheyenne, Sioux, Blackfeet, who, in his own successor world, had successfully stayed the advance of the European for a half century before going down to defeat under the steamroller of a civilization that would have no part of their virtues and talents. Here the Empire had assimilated, not crushed.

Only it was those very forces which the reactionary lords, who were rumored to be ready to rise against the mechanized civilization of the south, could depend upon for their backing. And they would have little reason to favor a captive from New Britain. These were tribesmen ever ready to raid across the frontier.

"Here. Go." Blake's special guard spoke English with a kind of disdain as he gave his captive a push to the left.

They emerged upon a narrow road to face quite an impressive company. Several yards away was a large car, not unlike the vans used in Port Ackrone. But this was half fort, half hunting camp. Mounted on its roof were three guns of a type strange to Blake. The side showed an open door, giving a glimpse of comfortable living quarters in the interior. And seated on a stool beside the door was the man who was the probable commander of the whole force.

His heavy nose and flattened forehead, elongating his skull, proved him to be one of the old noble families. But here in the wilderness he wore the tanned leather breeches, boots, and simple shirt of his men, although the badge on the latter was worked in gold thread. While his hunters carried blowpipes, he had a hand laser belted on, and the two men standing not too far away wore the uniforms of a private guard. They carried not only lasers but rifles as well. At the lord's feet lay the black jaguar, its gold and ruby collar bright.

An awning projecting from the side of the car kept the drizzle from the august person of the noble. Now the spotted cat bounded forward into that patch of dry, butting its head against the man's body. He fondled the fur about its ear, paying it all his attention with none left for the captive standing among his followers.

The two guards had the unmistakable features of the south, but the few words Blake caught were unintelligible. It was only after the two cats had been given bowls of food and were eating that the nobleman looked toward Blake, sweeping the wardsman with a gaze which missed not one tear, smear of river mud, or bruise.

He beckoned with a crooked finger, his attitude one of arrogance and contempt. For a fraction of a moment Blake wondered how this Imperial lordling would face Isin Kutur, for there was a certain similarity between them, civilizations, time streams, and worlds apart though they were.

"Where are you from?" the Toltecan drawled, but as if Blake's origin was really of little importance. One of the cats lifted its head and hissed.

"Port Ackrone, *Tecuhtli*," Blake gave the formal address due one of the old nobility. He could not fake an origin on this side of the river. Keep to the truth as much as he could; that was the wisest course. Though what means they might use to induce the whole truth out of a prisoner . . . Blake did not care to let his thoughts dwell upon that.

"So? That is well across the river and to the north. Then what do you here?"

"I was on a boat, bound for Xomatl. There was an accident and I fell overboard. When I reached shore, I did not know where I was—"

His guard made a sudden move which found Blake unprepared. He was pulled around and his bound arms jerked out so that the burn on the left could be exhibited to his questioner.

"An accident? You have been rayed, whiteskin. They say that the truth lies not within one of your kind, who speak with tongues that twist words instead of sending them straight for the hearing of honest men. But we have ways to having the truth out, even as the heart might go to Huitzilopochtli." His fingers moved in a sign, echoed by those around him.

"That you came from the river—that I can believe for you stink of it foully. Give me your name that we may send it downstream, you may be wanted."

"Rufus Trelawnly, of the Allowed Merchants, bound for Xomatl."

The noble spoke to one of the men behind him. "You have heard?" he asked in English as if he wanted Blake to understand.

"I have heard, *au cuch cabob*."

Councilor—with a Mayan title. Might he build anything on that? Blake wondered. The Mayans had been merchants first, exploring merchants. Could that bent have lingered on, making his supposed profession more acceptable than it would be to an Aztec war noble?

The man swung up into the forepart of the camp on wheels and Blake thought he was now broadcasting a report of the affair.

"So you are of the Allowed Merchants in Xomatl, where you doubtless have had dealings with *Yacabec, Pochteca Flatoque*." Now the Toltecan used Aztec rather than Mayan terms.

"With the *Pochteca Flatoque* does indeed my master have accord. I am not *Tecuhnenenque*. The name of the lord who is head of the merchants' guild is Npoaltzin."

The *ah cuch cabob* shrugged. He gave some order in the native tongue and Blake was urged on, past the camp to some other vehicles parked a short distance away, transportation for the rest of the party.

Several of those vans were equipped with cages built on their frames and two of these held occupants. One was a bear and the other a wolf of such size as to make Blake wonder if it would not be a

formidable opponent for one of the jaguars. Into a
third empty cage Blake was thrust. The enclosure
smelled vilely of some former inhabitant. The
wardsman sprawled on the dirty floor, trying to
steady himself as the motor came to life and the
truck backed onto roughly cleared space to turn
around.

They drove past the camp car.The nobleman
was rubbing the ears of one of the cats whose head
rested on his knee. He glanced up at the caged
Blake with a trace of smile that matched the snarl-
ing lip-lift of his pet.

The narrow forest track turned into a wide road,
this one with a surface of crushed stone, which, in
turn, became a highway paved with dressed stone
blocks. Now and then they passed other trucks
carrying supplies, but never anything Blake recognized as a passenger transport.

He was given nothing to eat or drink, though
the two women in the driver's cab, when they
paused at intervals to change places at the controls, shared out flatcakes of bread, made into
saucer-sized sandwiches with a dark paste between layers, and the contents of a bottle. By bracing his feet against the bars at the opposite side of
the cage, Blake managed to stay in a sitting position for some hours. But the constant tension of
that became more than he could endure, and at
last, the wardsman lay prone, his body all one
ache, striving only to protect his injured arm as he
was shaken about.

They passed through one small village along its
single street. Blake caught a glimpse of the river
flowing past a jetty. Their route was south, but
that was all he knew. And soon he did not care

about their final goal, only hoped they would
reach it while he still had some consciousness
left.

Darkness came as Blake fought off attacks of
lightheadedness which grew longer and more
sustained. He became aware of lights, of the fact
that the highway was now a street running between buildings which rivaled or overtopped
those of Port Ackrone. Flashes of light showed
that they were embellished with grotesque carv-
ings. And there was traffic, enough to make him
dizzy with the sounds of wheels and voices, all
the roar of a good-sized town.

Deeper dark closed about him, then light once
again, this time subdued, while the city sounds
came faintly. The truck halted and those on the
front seat got down. One stretched wide his arms
while the other called.

More voices, a greater degree of light. Then a
rattling at the door of the cage as it was flung back.
Hands caught at Blake, dragged him out. For all
his desire to front the enemy on his feet, the
wardsman sagged to the ground. A boot caught
him close to the burn, and that blow sent him
hurtling into unconsciousness.

Cold . . . wet . . . he was helpless in the river
. . . he was going to drown unless he fought.
Swim . . . move arms and legs . . . but he could
not. He was helpless in the current . . .

Water ran into his mouth, his hot, dry mouth.
Water—that was what he had wanted for so long.
The river was good. It would quench the fire inside him! Blake opened his mouth wider to drink,
but the fluid dashed against his flesh, not between
his parted lips.

Blake opened his eyes. There were faces hanging in the air above him. Three . . . four . . . none of them he knew. He tried to ask for water, his voice came as a rusty croaking. Hands in his armpits, jerking him up. Then the world spun and danced crazily. He shut his eyes because it made him sick to watch the spinning of the light, faces, and walls.

He could not walk, so he was dragged, his feet drumming helplessly as they pulled at him. And they were talking, but he could not understand one word they said. Then he was shoved forward, allowed to sprawl on a hard surface. He lay there gasping, until a boot toe was pushed under his body and he was rolled over on his back.

X

IT WAS HARD for Blake to open his eyes and focus on his surroundings. The bright light above him was searing, blanketing out the faces of his captors. Then one of them moved, dark eyes regarded him intently. A hand moved down, jerked at the heraldic buckle on his belt. There were sharp words, issuing what must be a series of orders.

Once more the wardsman was lifted and carried, but this time with a little more concern for him. And when he was dropped, it was onto a padding of mats. An old face, seamed with many wrinkles, swam out of the fog which now enclosed him. The sear burn was harsh pain, but his arms were free of bonds, leaden by his sides. His shoulders and head were raised; he was urged to drink from a bowl pressed against his lips. Bitter stuff which made him gag swilled about his mouth and finally got down his throat. He was lowered to the mats and he slept.

Blake came out of that sleep which had been dreamhaunted although he could not remember the dreams, into a sharpened awareness not only of his own mind and body, but also of his surroundings. This was precognition raised to the degree that he was a sounding board for varied impressions. Only once or twice before in his life had this happened, and each time he had drawn inner strength from that honing of the talent he possessed. A moment later as he lay there, eyes closed, giving no sign of his recovery, he felt that other thought thrusting in his mind, not such a probe as he had experienced among the men of Vroom, rather a kind of fumbling on the surface of his brain, as if the one who sought to read the secrets within his skull was not truly adept at this type of research.

He put up his briefed memories, those of Rufus Trelawnly. To select these and satisfy such a probe as this was easy, too easy. Suspicion throbbed through him with every beat of his heart. But he remained Rufus Trelawnly during that inquiry, until the clumsy seeker withdrew and he was alone in his own mind. Not—certainly not— any telepath from Vroom where such powers, trained and refined for generations, were as far beyond this clumsy invasion as the laser side-arm was beyond the obsidian-edged, wooden blades the men of the Empire had once carried into battle. But with people to whom any psi power was a wonder, the man who could read even surface thought would be a worker of magic. To this day, men of the Empire depended upon the *tonalpoulqui*—those practicing divination—and much of the privilege of their ancient priestly rank still held, especially among the lower classes. A man's horoscope, cast at birth, laid bare his life before he had breathed out his first few hours. And psi powers of any kind would make the *tonalpoulqui* possessing them notable and particularly reverenced.

Blake listened. No sound suggested that others were in the room. He opened his eyes, but did not move his head. Above him was white surface across which lay a bar of sunlight. Somewhere near there was cooking, for a spicy smell teased

his nostrils. The peace of those two observations
was belied by his warning.

He turned his head left and saw a wall, patterned with a mural of stylized flower-and-leaf
designs in gaudy colors, broken by three uncur-
tained windows. The panes were opaque, letting
through light but giving no sight of what lay
beyond.

A table stood by the wall, its surface only a short
distance from the floor. Those who used it must
sit crosslegged on the mats now piled together at
one end. From that he gained a scrap of knowledge; he was not in the quarters of any nobleman
but in a place where the owner kept the old customs now used only by the peasants.

His left arm was bandaged, heavy by his side.
With his right hand Blake explored the bed on
which he lay. Another pile of mats. And when he
turned his head right, he was fronted, only a foot
or so away, with a second painted wall. The torn,
wet clothing he had worn was gone. Now he was
covered with a rough shirt and a woven blanket of
bright colors and intricate designs.

He had been tended; he lay in a place that did
not appear to be a prison. So much was favorable.
For the rest, well, he had been warned, was being
alerted at this moment.

A cadenced tramping vibrated through the
floor under him. Blake sat up, put out a hand
against the painted wall to brace himself when the
room swung about him dizzily. As his head
cleared, he faced the door. Whoever stood on the
other side turning the key in the lock, for he heard
the grate of metal against metal, was to be feared.

The heavy door swung inward and Blake

looked up at the newcomer. He was a tall man
with the harsh, beaky features characteristic of the
old Aztec blood. His loose breeches were made of
a material worked with bands of fine embroidery,
red and blue. His full-sleeved shirt was of a clear
yellow with shoulder embellishments of embroidery. And his cloak had a boldly vivid feather
fringe. On his feet were calf-high boots fastened
with turquoise snaps, testifying to noble birth.
But it was not this resplendent visitor who had
unlocked the door. He held in his hand only a
bunch of flowers and herbs in a gemmed holder,
at which he sniffed now and then.

The key holder wore the uniform of a private
guard, and he was a plainsman not unlike those
who had formed the hunter-ranger party that had
captured Blake. He had a bundle under his arm
which he now tossed in the general direction of
the mat bed. It came apart in midair and Blake's
New Britain clothing cascaded out.

"Get up!" The guard accompanied that order
with a gesture to the clothing. "Dress. There is a
court."

Blake did not reach for the shirt lying within a
short distance. Boldness could be a weapon with a
warrior race.

"You speak of a court." He drew on the most
formal speech of New Britain for his reply. "That
is to say there has been a crime. Of what am I
accused?" He put a note of impatience in his voice
and repeated, "Of what am I accused, *Tecuhtli?*"
addressing himself not to the guard but his master. Nor did he miss the slight flaring in the nostrils of that prominent Aztec nose.

This lordling, whoever he might be, had not

expected such a reply. But the sooner he learned
Blake Walker owed him no "wood and water," the
better that might be. There had always been a
pessimistic acceptance of fate among those of the
ancient blood; they could be baffled by any refusal
to accept a decree. A people whose human sacrifices had once stood dutifully in line from sun-
rise to sunset, hundreds and even thousand of
them, marching dully and without struggle to the
fate of being cut open while yet living for the glory
of many gods, were not conditioned, even generations later, to defiance.

"Up!" The officer repeated his order. "The
Teactli waits!" He whistled and two soldiers appeared in the doorway behind the lord. "You
go—or they take you."

Blake reached for his clothing. It had been
roughly handled in addition to the damage suffered during his overland journey. Someone had
searched every seam, slit open any portion that
might have concealed something. For what had
they been hunting? At least the worst of the damage had been repaired with hasty, long stitches
which he hoped would hold together for the sake
of his own dignity if they were about to take him
into a court of law. As slowly as possible he
dressed.

One of the soldiers had vanished when it appeared that his services to button a recalcitrant
prisoner into his clothing were not needed. He
returned with a cup and bowl which he put down
on the table.

The officer gestured again. "Eat. Drink."

The contents of the cup was the ever-present
Toltec drink of chocolate, which, in this case, had

not been either spiced or flavored with vanilla.
But it was hot and, Blake knew, sustaining. The
bowl held maize cakes, spread very thinly with a
paste which gave some relief to their dryness. He
ate and drank to the last crumb and drop. If they
were indeed taking him to a court, they would
have him out in the city. He continued to specu-
late even when his good sense told him there was
no hope of escape in this unknown city where his
skin, his hair, his clothing marked him as surely
as if he carried a banner in one hand inscribed "I
am an escaped prisoner."

Having seen him clothed and fed, the noble
stalked out, his bouquet of flowers used rather as a
rod of office, which its stiff, ceremonial arrangement did not deny. The officer strode behind him,
while Blake between two soldiers brought up the
rear. They entered a narrow-roofed and walled
passage. Through a gate-opening Blake caught a
glimpse of a garden, riotous in color. But he had
more attention for the man waiting at the end of
the passage where it gave upon a courtyard holding several vehicles.

This—this was the would-be mind reader! As a
hound might scent a natural enemy in one of the
great cats, so Blake's warning gave him notice
now. The man was older than the nobleman, having the same Aztec features except that these were
harshened even more by a tightly set mouth and
eyes sunk beneath bony skull ridges. His hair,
threaded with dull gray, was worn longer, matted,
dull, looking as if it had gone uncombed for years,
some of it sticking into points. Unlike the others,
his clothing was black, his coat so long it resembled a robe. He leaned on a polished staff which

bore faint indentations and curves, as if it had once been carved and the carving had been worn away by centuries of handling.

The noble stepped quickly to one side, showing this oldster the same deference his own men displayed toward him. And the officer pressed himself gainst the wall of the passage as he waved Blake on to face the old man. The wardsman, meeting those deep-set eyes, knew that what he saw in them was nothing which could be a part of any sane life. The alert of his warning was reinforced by an inward repulsion, an uncontrollable shrinking.

Vroom and its people had been alien to the world in which he lived during childhood and early manhood. On other levels he had seen "people" far different from his kind, whose life patterns had varied from the road he walked until they had little or nothing in common. He had caught breaths of what was to him the rank depths of evil, a kind of evil few of his breed had ever plumbed. But here was something still different: a fanaticism rooted not only in this man but in generations upon generations behind him. He was not a man as Blake reckoned his fellows, but rather an incarnation of dark purposes, a vessel which held a power or desire or will, that was no longer human, if it ever had been.

He was power, dark power. And as he looked at Blake, he was also hunger, a hunger long denied. The inner warning in the wardsman became a need for flight, so great that Blake thought he could never control it. For a long time, or so it seemed to the younger man, they stood looking at one another. Then the staff in the oldster's hand moved, its time-smoothed top tapped Blake on the breast. The lightest of touches, and yet the wardsman felt as if the worn wood had in that instant laid some smarting brand upon him.

Without a word the man in black turned, shuffled across the courtyard and climbed stiffly into one of the cars. His use of that means of transportation was incongruous, out of character. And the mere fact he did so broke the spell for Blake. But now he was also being propelled by his guard into the back of a small van.

There were windows in the van but they were latticed, so that any glimpse he had of the streets through which they passed was fragmentary. But it was intended for passengers, since it was furnished with surprisingly comfortable and well-cushioned seats, one of which Blake shared with two guards planted firmly on either side. Nor did either man speak.

The Empire had a high form of justice; that much Blake had learned during his studies. And from the remote past the courts had been incorruptible; the penalty for any partiality was death for the judge. But why they would bring him under their jurisdiction Blake could not understand. Anyone in his predicament was usually declared a spy and turned over to the army for very summary justice, with perhaps a "hearing" that was really an interrogation, during which the prisoner might die and so save any more bother on the part of his captors. But apparently he was on his way to one of the legal courts. And the reason for that?

To prevent an "incident" which might cause trouble with New Britain? Blake doubted that.

Both nations had operated for years now on the basis that their nationals traveled across the border at their own risk, and that they might expect no aid from home should those risks prove a trap.

The car turned a corner and came to a stop, the back door clanged open. Blake blinked his way into brilliant sunlight. He stood at the pavement end of an imposing flight of stairs, leading up three flights, to a building set on a pyramid base. The monumental ruins that had been found in jungles on his own successor world, ruins that awed travelers and explorers three, four, five centuries after they ceased to mark living cities, were the forerunners of this civic structure. The feathered serpents, jaguars, and god masks that had ornamented those in profusion had in the course of time become more symbolic designs. But the fine stonework still remained.

If Blake had something to stare at in the building and the brightly dressed crowd about him, so did the latter gather to gaze back at him. A volley of orders sent guards to clear the stairway. The wardsman might have been one of the Emperor's staff, judging by the speed in which that operation was carried out. Even nobles pressed back to open a path.

The stairs were steep, the treads narrow. Blake's guards kept step with him, either as supports or deterrents against some last-minute bid for freedom. Then they came through a pillared outer way into the interior.

The inner room was crowded, too. No trial in the Empire was by jury; verdict was rendered by a panel of judges who sat on a platform in the old way, crosslegged on mats. Behind them was yet

another dais for the Imperial power. Centering
that stood a bench carved with the legs of a jaguar,
fanged heads marking the arm rests, cushioned by
a mat of woven eagle feathers. Thus it stood, always waiting for a time when the Emperor might
see fit to visit his court.

Now there was a scrambling hurry to clear a
way to the judges' seat, that path lined with uni-
formed men. Blake was brought to a stand directly
before the platform, his guards falling back a few
steps to leave him conspicuously alone. A court
official began a droning speech, consulting at intervals a roll that had been handed him. Now and
again one of the judges nodded during a pause in
the drone or made a comment. When the speaker
had come to an end, they all looked at Blake as if
expecting something from him in return. Well, he
could at least ask for an explanation. Some of
them must understand English, even if they did
not choose to advertise the fact.

"May it please the court"—that was the first so-
lution which came to him as proper—"I do not
know what charge has been laid against me. Am I
not to know the crime for which I am being tried?"

There was a moment of silence and then one of
the judges spoke, his English bearing only the
slightest of accents.

"You have appealed to the justice of the Great
One. He of the Feather Scales." The judge bowed
his head. "You have been accused before this
court and the Throne of the Great One of—"

He was interrupted by a stir in the hall behind
Blake. Change! His precognition told him that.
There was a change coming. He was trying to
assess the meaning in this warning and did not

look behind. On his left those in the body of the
hall were pressing yet farther back. More soldiers
filed into line. These wore scarlet cloaks and the
jaguar-mask duty helmets of the elite corps. One
of them, an officer by the plumed crest, leaped to
the upper dais reserved for the Emperor, and
draped a cloak of dramatic black and white over
the cushion.

It was the sign of the *Cuiacoatl*, the Vice-
Emperor, who had only one superior in the whole
of Toltec territory, and that the boy Emperor himself. But the man who mounted the dais with
deliberate tread was no boy. He was perhaps in his
late thirties and not a warrior such as those who
paid him deference. For he walked with a rocking,
sidewise gait caused by a shortened left leg, and
his left arm was carefully hidden in the folds of
his cloak of state, while his face closely resembled
one of the crystal skulls jewelers of the Empire
carved with such exquisite and detailed precision.

This was Tlacaclel, the eldest brother of the late
Emperor, passed over for the rulership because of
his physical infirmities, but whose mental
abilities had made such a mark on the circle of
close councilors that they had been at last forced
to grant him the vice-rulership, however much
they disliked the doing. Having settled himself on
the throne, he nodded sharply to his officer who
brought the butt of a ceremonial "presence" spear
crashing down on the stone.

Blake thought he saw the faintest of shivers
hunch the shoulders of the judge now seated directly before the person of that crippled royal
hawk. But without otherwise acknowledging

the presence of the *Cuiacoatl*, the judge began his indictment for the second time.

"You have been brought here, Stranger, charged with seeking to ferret out the secrets of the Emperor's house, striving to cause trouble—"

The *Cuiacoatl* stared down at Blake. As the judge paused, he spoke abruptly. "What story has this over-the-river one given to explain himself?"

The judges all stirred. *Cuiacoatl* or not, living presence of the Emperor or not, this pushing aside of orderly procedure in the court was forbidden.

Tlacaclel gestured again, and once more the spear butt ordered silence and attention. Now the Vice-Emperor pointed a long nailed forefinger directly at Blake.

"Speak you. What is your tale?"

The truth, as far as it would go, Blake decided swiftly. He was depending a great deal on his new warning signal: expect change but not outright danger.

"I am of the Allowed Merchant company bound for Xomatl according to the law, Great One . . ." He made a short story of it though he spoke slowly. His fall from the boat was edited into an accident, but for the rest he kept to the facts. How much of it was understood by his listeners he did no know, although most of the nobles and the merchant class understood English.

As he talked, Blake's mind worked. One of the many facts he had learned on Vroom came to mind. When he had done, he stooped, touched his finger to the floor, and then to his lips, before he again faced the Vice-Emperor. "This do I swear by Huitzilopochtli!"

Five hundred years ago a man speaking so could never be questioned further as to the truth of what he said. Tlacaclel studied him for a moment before he answered.

"Since the Butterfly One has ceased to hold the promise of life or death in this land, Stranger, you indeed swear strangely. But still I think the need with which those words were once summoned continues to carry weight. Is there anyone you may call now to speak for you, give bond that you are what you say, to be returned to your countrymen as having meant to do no evil to this land or those who dwell therein? Who in the hearing of the judges will so speak?"

Was that question really addressed to Blake? The *Cuiacoatl* was no longer watching the prisoner, his attention swept for a telling second to the throng who stood walled away by the guards on Blake's right.

"This one so speaks."

An officer moved to the fore of the crowd. He was not one of the wearers of the Jaguar badge, his uniform was plain amid all that spread of color. And Blake did not recognize the insignia on the breast of his jacket.

"Let it be recorded that the worthy Cuauhuehuetque of the border, Thohtzin, has spoken for the prisoner, knowing that he swears to the truth of this stranger and that guilt or innocence is now equal for both!"

The *Cuiacoatl* spoke swiftly and again the judges stirred. But no one objected openly. Thohtzin stepped up to the lower dais, made some formal declaration which the others responded to, and then came directly to Blake, the guards standing aside though with visible reluctance.

"Come quickly!"

Blake needed no urging. He did not know what lay behind this, but his luck had taken a change for the better and he was willing to ride on it for now. At any rate, he went free where he had come under guard.

XI

IT WAS NOT until they drove out on a wharf that Blake knew they had been heading for the river, since Thohtzin made no explanation and the wardsman thought it wise not to ask questions until he was surer of his ground. Their car was driven by a soldier in the same plain uniform as the officer wore, and there were two more men on the seat behind.

Tied up at the wharf was a small cruiser, one man standing at her controls, another waiting to cast off mooring ropes. For the second time Thohtzin ordered: "Come quickly!"

He pushed Blake ahead of him into the boat, glancing back up the street as if fearing to see active pursuit. It was not until they were moving into the main current of the river at a speed exceeding any Blake had seen used by water-borne traffic that the officer relaxed.

He touched the wardsman on the arm, motioning him toward the wheelhouse where he himself relieved the man on duty, taking the steering mechanism into his hands. When they were left alone, he half smiled at Blake.

"Truly you must have set out on your travels on One of the Snake, or else you were born under that favorable sign, Teyaualouanimi. We are not yet beyond a flight of darts, should those who wish you to meet Xipi or Huitzilopochtli after the old fashion move to enforce that desire. Only the Great One could so overrule the will of the

Tlalogue thus. By the Nine, what ill wind brought you into this?"

Feel your way carefully, Blake warned himself. Obviously he was being taken for someone who had reason to claim aid from some of the Emperor's subjects. Was that true of the real Rufus Trelawnly?

"It was as I told the judges," he replied. "A fall from the ship—"

"Which left you scorched by a ray?" The glance at him this time was far more measuring.

"That happened after I hit the water," Blake said. "I do not know who fired at me, or why."

It was a good guess, that answer, for the officer was nodding.

"Yes, that could well be. For seeing you in the river, the guards would only follow their regular orders, and Ah Kukum dared not countermand them without bringing suspicion on us. Nactitl's eyes and ears ply those boats, both openly and secretly. Tell me, how goes the negotiations? You have good news?"

Blake looked at the swirling water through which the bow of the cruiser was cutting a swift course. "The last I heard all was proceeding smoothly. My—my superior would know more." Ambiguous, but again he apparently satisfied his questioner.

"The day . . ." Thohtzin raised one hand from the wheel, brought it down clenched into a fist. "Ah, the day when once more we can raise the standards, sound the shell trumpets!" He paused and shot Blake a look of what might be embarrassment. "That is only speaking in the old terms—we do not fight as did our forefathers."

"The courage of the Empire is well known, also the skill of her soldiers, and their ability," Blake agreed.

"Of which there shall be soon a good showing! This new law they force upon us, no more defenses, an opening of the border. Trade, ever trade . . ."

What did he mean, Blake wondered. The story at Ackrone had been of tightening of controls, of unrest aimed at perhaps eventual reopening of hostilities between the two nations. Yet here was the hint of a striving for more liberal policy.

"Tell me," Thohtzin went on, "why is it you English wish to pull down those of New Britain, make them meat for the Empire?"

That was a good question and a baffling one. Somehow Blake found words. "When have there never been factions under any rule? I am only a soldier in the ranks; to such problems my superior may have a reply."

Again Thohtzin was off on another track. "Tell me, have you seen these new weapons with your own eyes, these sounds which can shake a stone wall into rubble, bring men screaming out of any fort with no weapons in their hands, only the need to flee? And that which, when a man breathes it in the air, makes his mind an empty thing so that he will stand unknowing while his enemies march past the gate he is set to guard? Have you seen these?"

Blake groped for the edge of the windbreak before him. He was as shocked as if he had taken the full force of a laser ray dead center, save this was cold and deadly, not roasting heat.

"Yes . . ." That began as a whisper. He forced

his voice higher. "Yes, I have seen such weapons!" He gazed at the water, but he did not see that, nor the cruiser, nor Thohtzin. Rather Blake drew from memory the screening of a record tape as shown in corps instruction in Vroom.

The world had had a dark and bloody history. On all the successor levels except those on which mankind had never come into being, war, rumors of war, battle and defeat, had been the way of life. Far earlier than his own successor world, Vroom had climbed to a mechanically based civilization, planet-wide. Mechanical and then atomic and then—the last blazing, terrible war sending remnants of the human race into barbarism save for small pockets of survivors. Out of that weltering chaos had come a three-quarters dead world and, eventually, the saving crosstiming. In the last frenzied days of a dying civilization, fearsome weapons had been devised, some never put to use. But they were known, their results indelibly impressed on each and every descendant of those who had been mad enough to create them. Vroom was now a peaceful level, but still there was constant surveillance so as to be sure that no warped personality could threaten that peace. Yet here, on another level, a man talked familiarly of some of those outlawed weapons! This could only leak from Vroom. No other successor world had crosstime travel, and the level in which they now were did not have the technology to produce such devices.

"You find these weapons indeed awesome, Teyaualouanimi?"

"They are of the devil!" Blake exploded, and then was too well aware of his self-betrayal.

"Devil?"

"Of great evil."

"Perhaps. But sometimes one accepts aid from the *tztizimime*, the ancient monsters of the twilight, to bring about good. For what will become of our way of life if these *tecuhnenenque*, who think more of their treasures than of their honor and that of the Great Serpent, take from us our arms and so make of us slaves? Also, we need not use such weapons, or perhaps only once, to show what we have. Then shall those who would pour poison into the water which we drink be as dogs and run about barking, knowing no safe place in which to hide. To have a keen sword in one's hand and the ability to use it makes a man walk tall and the lesser give him careful room!"

How much of that was true belief, Blake speculated, and how much the sugar-coating they were conditioned to accept?

"We would not give such arms into the hands of the extremists."

"The extremists?"

Thohtzin smiled. "You may now speak with the authority of one who has had a meeting with them. The Lord Chacxib who had you brought to judgment gives harborage, and more than half an ear, to Ihuitimal, who in the old days would have been a *cuacuacuiltin*, one of the venerable Old Ones consecrated to Huitzilopochtli. I have heard him speak concerning the wishes of his heart. *Cuauhuehuetque* was once not a title given to those who hold dangerous duty on the frontiers. It meant then a fighting priest of the first rank. Perhaps you of England do not study our history well enough to understand the meaning. . . ."

"I know a little," Blake responded as the other paused.

"Then you must know that ours was once a most bloody, as you would say, way of life. For each fighting man was dedicated to the capture, not the killing, of the enemy so that those captives might be given to the gods. And we had many gods, all thirsty for the livers of men. Only through the capture of many enemies might a man rise to honor, and that stairway was open to the humblest and not just to men whose fathers had been great before them.

"There are those who have always turned to the old gods and their ways, who repudiated the wishes of Quetzalcoatl when he first came to substitute grain, birds, flowers for the human hearts on the sacrifice stones. And when the second Kukulcán arose with the same message, there were those who defied him to the last, keeping alive the old ways in secret.

"Now they begin to emerge from the shadows of secrecy, attach themselves to the party of the Return. And since every man means so much more support, they are welcome to fight on our side. But once the battle is over, the extremists will not find their dream of bloodsmoking altars brought alive. Meanwhile, they are not crossed too much. Had the judgment gone against you . . ."

Again the officer paused and looked sidewise at Blake, that moment of silence lengthening until the wardsman prompted: "Then what might have happened?"

"You could have been returned to the Lord Chacxib, on whose land you were taken, for him to render justice. And that would have brought you into the hands of Ihuitimal and his followers, to feed the god they invoke."

Varlt's fear for Marva! If Thohtzin could seriously suggest this, then Varlt had good reason for his fears. The wardsman strove to appear impassive, his tone one of interest only as he asked. "This *does* happen?"

"It does." Thohtzin's expression was one of disgust. "They say we must bind the extremists to us because they control the villagers and the wild men. The honor of warriors is a good thing, it is the lifeblood of the Empire, but one cannot recall the past. We should not trouble the sleep of old gods. Once we have these new weapons, then none, priest or merchant, will dare walk against us."

"We shall dock at Xomatl at dawn," he added a moment later. "Once you are again with your people you must tell your superior that we have no time to waste. The girl is safe, but how long she remains hidden without talk we cannot tell. No matter how one stops all cracks in any women's quarters, still gossip and rumor run like open streams into the city, and this is a tale worth repeating many times over. Therefore, let your party move soon lest you find you have nothing to bargain with and no one to blame but yourselves."

"I will do so."

Marva! She must be "the girl." But who—who was Rufus Trelawnly's superior? The merchant Varlt was now impersonating in Xomatl? Surely, if the Allowed Merchants were connected with a crosstime outlaw, Arshalm would have known —or suspected—as much. Unless he, too, was a part of the whole. This affair continued to widen

out like the ripples from a stone thrown into a
pool. Perhaps the wardsmen's team was on the
edge of something far too great for the small force
to handle.

Thohtzin summoned the wheelsman, and they
went below to eat better rations than Blake had yet
tasted this side of the river. Afterward the Imperial officer flung himself on a mat-filled bunk and
signed Blake to take the one across the cabin. Even
as the wardsman settled himself on the couch, he
could hear the even breathing of his cabinmate,
but his own slumber was light, a series of dozes
from which he continued to awake, remembering
and worrying.

A mist clung along the river banks in the very
early morning. The speed of the cruiser had been
sharply reduced as they approached the city. Save
for a few scattered lights, the bulk of the buildings
silhouetted against the sky was dark. And no one
stirred along the dock where they moored with a
precision that suggested that this might not be the
first surreptitious run the craft had made to this
port.

If any watchman had been stationed on the
wharf, he was now elsewhere. Blake hurried
along, trying to keep pace with Thohtzin. They
sped the length of the jetty and then across a
quayside street to a warehouse. A dim light over a
small door set into a larger portal illuminated the
entrance Thohtzin used.

The interior was filled with cargo, boxed and in
tall baskets. At regular intervals along the high
roof, lights burned, giving Blake a view of the
Imperial officer on the move down the middle
aisle between two walls of goods. They were al-

most to the far end when Thohtzin halted and began counting a row of baskets. When his finger touched one, he made the count again, this time from the other end of the line, as if to make doubly sure of his choice. Then he busied himself with the fastening and lifted the cover.

"In," he whispered. "You wait. Make no sound if you would ever get to your friends."

In the bottom of the basket were folded cloths which Thohtzin pulled up, packing them around Blake as the wardsman crouched, his arms about his bent knees, in the container. A second or so later the lid fell, leaving him a few cracks for communication with the outer world. He heard the soft fumbling of Thohtzin making tight the fastenings once again.

After that, nothing but silence and a growing cramp in his arms and legs. He might have dozed again, his forehead resting on his knees, for he roused to sound: talking, some calls, the purr of machinery.

There was conversation in the Toltec tongue just outside the basket. Then, without further warning, the basket was swung through space and was lowered again. What it rested on moved. Blake was too far from any of the light- and air-permitting cracks to see anything, but he was sure they had come out of the warehouse into the open. Another swing, and once more the basket was deposited on another surface. Abruptly the light was gone, the vibration of a motor shook him.

He could deduce nothing from the confusion of muffled sound. The basket swayed a little now and then as if the van rounded curves. Then they halted; a third swing through air, jamming him against one side of the rough basket with no chance of avoiding the bruising impact, and again he was set down with jarring force.

"That is the last of the lot." Words spoken in English! And the voice was that of one of the wardsmen pulled in to make up the last minute recruitment of the team! But was he alone? Dare Blake strive to draw his attention?

"Might as well open them up then . . ."

Lo Sige! That was Lo Sige!

Remembering the other's present cover, Blake called, "Richard—Richard Wellford!" His dust-dry voice did not sound very loud to him. But there was instant silence without. Then the lid was unfastened, lifted. Blake strove to raise his hands to the edge of the container. It swayed and fell forward so that he lay half in, half out, on a stone floor.

Hands grasped his shoulders and drew him up, although it seemed for an instant that his numbed legs might not bear his weight. Lo Sige, yes, and the other wardsman who had helped Blake store cargo—how many days ago?

"Quite a delivery." As cool as ever, Lo Sige's voice broke the silence first. "Cargo slightly damaged, but still intact, I would say. How damaged and—how intact?"

What he might mean by the last Blake had no idea. He dropped the hand he had extended to grip Lo Sige's arm, ashamed at that show of his intense relief. Wih Lo Sige he was most wary of any display of emotion. The other's habitual detachment divorced him from such weakness, making any such the more apparent when a companion revealed it.

Blake tried to match Sige's control. "A laser burn for damage, otherwise intact. Where is Master Frontnum?" At least he remembered to ask for Varlt by his cover name.

"Aloft. But," Lo Sige appeared pensive, "we have our own resident eyes and ears working for the Emperor. To get you above without too much remark presents a small problem. Ah, a good trick may be worked twice! We have found some grievous damage in shipment, Henry," he said to the other wardsman, "almost suggesting deliberate spoilage. To be certain, the shipment must be examined by our master in its entirety. Back into the basket, Rufus. Then we'll see how clever we can be with our own trans-shipment."

Not daring to disagree, Blake re-entered the constrained prison. There followed a great deal of grunting and shifting, bruise-raising contacts with the side of the basket. Eventually they came to a halt and Blake heard Lo sige's low-pitched voice.

"As I said, Master Frontnum, malicious damage, surely malicious damage. A deposition must be made as we unpack. I am certain the insurance will cover this, but we should have proof."

"We shall see." Varlt sounded pontifical, the very assured master of the party, allowing no one to make decisions for him or influence his thinking. The lid lifted once again and with far less than his usual agility, Blake climbed out.

"A very novel entrance." Varlt's comment echoed Lo Sige's. "I think that it is in order we have a sharing of knowledge. Sit down, man. Richard?"

"Right here." Lo Sige materialized beside

Blake, steering him to one of the stools serving as chairs, putting into his hand a cup which gave off the aromatic odor Blake knew from Vroom, an energizing stimulant that acted as a quick restorative.

"Now." Varlt had waited until half the liquid was down Blake's throat before he continued. "Suppose we hear just what happened to you since you went out on deck five nights ago."

Blake reported, carefully. There was no recorder for his words as there had been in Vroom, but he knew that both men, when he had done, could give back the substance of his report almost word for word. He made it as quick as he could, but he wanted to leave out no significant detail. And neither commented, even when he paused for more sips of the stimulant.

"Maze within maze within maze," Lo Sige observed when he had done.

Varlt plucked at the pointed beard which was the bushy identity mark for Master Frontnum.

"So they believed you to be a contact with an arms runner." He spoke as if arranging his thoughts aloud. "Yet nothing turned up during our combing of the memories of this merchant group to explain that, not a hint of anything save the legal trade. And not one of them was shielded, either."

"That password you did not respond to—which error sent you into the river—" Lo Sige said, "someone expected you, or a contact, to be aboard the boat. And they would not have taken a chance on the wrong man. Therefore, they expected, if not the real Rufus Trelawnly, a counterfeit double. Which would also explain the prompt action to get rid of you. I would wager that substitution is not exclusively our game here. We merely got in first!"

"And they did not expect us to ask any betraying questions when you turned up here again." Varlt gazed into space. "This needs thinking about. As you say, Richard, the tangle grows more twisted as we advance. I see a number of loops but no ends. Rufus, let Worsley see your arm, then rest up."

So definitely was that an order Blake dared not dispute his summary dismissal. Also, he was glad that the decisions were no longer all his. With the years of experience behind him, Varlt's choice of action should be the better.

XII

"MARVA IS HERE AT—as far as we have been able to discover—the estate of one Otorongo who holds a unique position. It has been only for the past hundred years that the crown has descended by primogeniture. In the old days the Emperor's brothers or nephews were more eligible to succeed him than his sons. The crown was, in effect, an elective office rather than rule by divine right or inheritance. This Otorongo is a descendant of one of the earlier emperors, so possesses those ill-defined rights which every offshoot of royalty can claim in a kingdom. He has always been considered a dilettante uninterested in politics, the foremost patron of the goldsmiths, with numerous protegés in the arts, stages a concert once a year which is famous in this province. Now, in preparing for the fifty-two-year cycle he is planning a very elaborate series of both private and public entertainments."

"No tie with the military party?" Lo Sige asked when Varlt had finished.

Varlt pushed a fingertip eraser-fashion back and forth across the map of the city which lay on the table.

"When you have only superficial talk and rumor to depend on for information, you are not sure of anything. Outwardly his interests are as I have said. What under-the-cover-of-night allegiances he maintains, who can tell?"

"Marva is there," Marfy stared down at the map, "and we are here." She stabbed a forefinger down less than an inch away from the point Varlt had indicated. But that inch represented no small distance in the city. "We must get her out!"

Varlt did not list the difficulties in such action, nor did he look up from the map he continued to smooth.

"Day after tomorrow is the beginning of the cycle. Strangers from the country are pouring into the city for the rites and general festivities after the kindling. This is one time that men may come and go unseen or undetected. Otorongo could well use his entertainment as a cover for meetings, if that is what he desires. And so . . ."

Blake stirred. "Thohtzin and whoever is behind him believed me to be their contact with this supplier of off-level arms. Could we play on that for a chance to reach Marva?"

Varlt raised his eyes, gave the younger man a long, measuring survey.

"It might have had a chance had he given you any point of contact here in Xomatl, if you knew where to locate him. But—"

"But—but—and again but!" Marfy burst out. "I tell you, I know where Marva is. I can find her within an hour. Then, with her safe here—"

"With her here—in the Allowed Merchant's quarters?" Varlt's eyebrows raised, his tone was cold. "This is the first place they would search and we have no way of retreat. There is only one chance. We must put to use the excitement of these cycle days to cover our moves. To withdraw overland would merely set hunters on our trail at once. We shall have to get a launch or river boat, be sure of that. And then, once our escape is ready, move suddenly, perhaps with only a single chance of action."

Blake rose and walked to the far wall of the room where a mirror hung, reflecting the company about the table. But he was more intent upon the image of his own face.

The radical cosmetic treatments of the Vroom technicians had lightened his skin and it would remain so if he applied the proper creams. But he had neglected to do that since his arrival in Xomatl, and the days of his captivity had already started the reversal process. He had seen lords coming in to inspect the goods on the lower shop floor whose skin was the color of his own. And, while the strong features of the Aztec and Mayan ruling caste were sharply distinguishable, he had confidence that wardsman techniques could provide those also for a short period.

Varlt's eyes met his in the mirror. Blake thought that the senior wardsman was quite able to read if not his mind, then his intentions.

"A hunter from the north could be one of the visiting strangers?" Blake made a question of that.

"To do what?" demanded Varlt bluntly.

"To try his luck at finding Thohtzin."

"Or Marva!" Marfy was on her feet. "It is right . . . get her out . . . maybe hide along the river to be picked up . . ."

"Thohtzin," Varlt repeated thoughtfully, paying no attention to the girl. "And if you find him, then what? Also, you have no briefing on the actions of a northern hunter. You could betray yourself in the first five minutes in any of fifty different ways."

"The streets are crowded, strangers are many. Choose a distant native place for me." Blake had no feeling of excitement, rather did purposeless waiting wear harder on him. And since this idea had come into mind, he had had no precognition warning. So, for the present at least, there was no danger in this.

"Say you do find him"—Lo Sige now played the devil's advocate—"what do you do?"

"Invite him here, for a meeting with my superior."

Varlt's finger no longer rubbed the map. Now he alternately crooked and straightened it as if beckoning to someone unseen.

"You are thinking that Thohtzin has access to a fast cruiser as well as information that we would be well advised to hear?"

"That's about it."

"Thohtzin," Varlt mused. "I wish we knew a little more about him. The zin name ending is honorary, and the name itself means 'hawk.' His rank is cuauhuehuetque—fighting priest— though that is an old title applied to a new service with a different connotation entirely. And where would you begin to look for this high-flying hawk?"

"Where I saw him last, on the docks. If the cruiser is still there—"

Lo Sige laughed. "We, who are supposed to be cautious, secretive, and all the rest, appear now to be playing the wildest of chances. Oh, don't look to me! I have nothing better to offer."

The hour was past the high of noon as Blake followed on the heels of a party drifting out of the show room on the lowest floor of the Allowed Merchants' house. There were guards at the portal, but they had not prevented the entrance of wealthy merchants and nobles eager to look over the imports, nor did they appear to check too closely on those who left; the relaxed feeling of holiday apparently was at work already. The party from New Britain could do no trading on its own, of course, only through the intermediaries provided by the city guilds.

Once in the street, Blake paused to study the landmarks. He had a good quarter of the city to cross before reaching the wharves. One of the cars for hire might pick him up; best to walk on before trying that.

A man brushed past him, thrust something into his hand. Blake controlled his desire to look until he raised his hand as if to adjust his broad-brimmed hunter's hat: a feather, barred dark on light. Again he faced the dilemma of not being able to read what should have been a plain message. But at least he had not lost sight of the messenger, and since he was headed in the same direction, Blake followed him.

It began to seem that the messenger intended to be followed. He chose, or appeared to choose, open spaces in the crowd now and then, as if seeking to remain in Blake's sight. And they continued to walk in the general direction of the wharves.

No unengaged "for hire" vehicle passed. Blake watched the red turban of the man he trailed. His headgear resembled that worn by all household servants, save that there was no family crest plainly visible against the scarlet cloth. And the violent hue, so easy to spot, was not unusual in this city where bright colors were more the rule than the exception. As Blake watched, the man in the turban slipped out of the main stream of the passing crowd into a narrow space between two

buildings. Reaching that point in turn, Blake hesitated. No warning from his private signal. Discre-
tion dictated that he keep on to the wharf. He had
only a feather in his hand and the suspicion that
he had been deliberately guided. Suddenly that
was enough to have him take one of those risks Lo
Sige had foreseen. He went into the alley.

Windowless walls cast a slice of shadow in the
sunny day. No sign of red turban, either. But there
was a door in the passage, two of them: one at the
end of the passage, the other halfway down the
wall on Blake's right. His quarry might have used
either and Blake did not propose to knock to find
out.

He was about to turn back when there was
movement in one of the shadowed doorways; the
door was swinging in silent invitation. Blake
waited for his inner warning, but that did not fire
in direct alarm. Soft-footedly he walked the
length of that dark strip to the now half-open
door.

As he stepped inside he found himself facing
the man from whom Thohtzin had taken the
wheel during their river voyage.

"The *Cuauhuehuetque*." Though he wore civilian dress now he was still unmistakably a soldier by bearing as he flattened against the wall
and jerked a thumb left along the narrow hall in
which they now stood. Blake went, hearing behind him the sound of a bolt being shot. If he had
walked into a trap, its first defenses were now
sprung, but his warning was quiet and he did not
look back.

He entered a storeroom filled with strange
smells of food he could not identify; other odors

floated in around another door. Beyond, there was the hum of muffled noise which suggested activity.

"Here."

The limited light did not hide the man rising from a seat on a box. Thohtzin indeed, but not as Blake had seen him last. His smart uniform had been exchanged for that of a private soldier from the north. And he wore the traces of face paint some of the frontier tribes affected, which helped mask his features. Instead of an officer's laser, a long knife, guarded by a bead-decorated sheath, rested across his thigh. For a moment or two he studied Blake and then nodded.

"Clever enough, if you do not talk to the wrong man. This day will find more of your chosen disguise in Xomatl than normally walk her streets. Yes, it will serve very well."

"For what?" asked Blake and then wondered if such a question had been wise.

"There is trouble." Thohtzin plunged in at once. "The eyes and ears on the riverboat. One of them reported your mishap, but said you died in the river. With your return—and do not doubt that has already been reported, too—there will be questions asked. But time is against them, even as it hampers us. That forked-tongue frog, Otorongo, is croaking again. He has been experimenting with the Sacred Smoke. Sacred Smoke!" Thohtzin spat the words. "We are no longer ignorant believers in all the priests tell us. A man using that sees, not visions sent by the gods who died when men ceased to believe in them, but fancies buried in his own mind, which, when he prates them to the recording priests, can be twisted in any fashion the listener chooses to set them. But once a man becomes caught in those murky 'mysteries,' then he is ripe for any suggestion whispered into his ears. Otorongo has always been a seeker of new sensations, or old ones he has not yet tasted. Since he has begun to drink smoke, he is drawn to some better forgotten, and he cannot be trusted.''

"Thus?" Blake prompted as the other paused.

"Thus it is best that he no longer be allowed possession of the girl."

"You will take her away?"

Thohtzin shook his head. "No. You shall."

"Why? And how?"

"Why? Because she is rightfully the possession of those who would bargain for us, as they have told us since they first hid her here. And since you speak for them, you can also see that she must not be risked before her usefulness to us is past. And how? That shall also be your doing—in part. Otorongo throws open his garden this afternoon to the people of the city. Since it is the end of *Xiuhlolpilli*, he is minded to make a great gesture to amaze men more than anything else he has done before. He would allow his pleasure garden, the outer one, to be ravaged, devastated, before building it anew. All in the city are bidden to rob him of any treasure growing there. You will be there two hours before sunset. Slip over the wall before the gates are thrown open. Once in, you must cross to the inner way leading to the pleasure garden for those in the house of women. For the rest," Thohtzin smiled grimly, "it will be your doing. Those of the household keeping watch on the girl will have their drink spiced with new herbs, this is all I can promise you."

Blake could hardly believe this stroke of luck. He mistrusted it as being too easy. Yet . . .

"Something else," he watched Thohtzin closely, "we will need a way of escape. The Merchants' house will be suspect—"

"Otorongo cannot accuse anyone without dirtying his own shield."

"You think he will accept her disappearance without a fight?"

Thohtzin grinned. "That depends upon the mood he is in, how far he will go. What do you want?"

"A boat—say, one like your cruiser—to get away."

"To go where?" The grin disappeared. Thohtzin once more was grim under his paint.

"You name the destination, send your own guards if you will," Blake offered. Given so much of a chance, he did not doubt the efficiency of the wardsmen in making use of opportunity.

"I will have to consult my superior concerning that."

"What did you have in mind?" Blake asked and then added, "It would be very easy for Otorongo's guards to deal with us both, would it not? His prisoner, since he could no longer keep her, and the stranger who strove to steal her?"

"Well thought!" Thohtzin applauded. "Only you forget this, the girl is still necessary to our plans. Not so necessary that my superior dares reveal his identity in order to bring her forth by his own men, but enough so that we will not leave her to Otorongo's caprices. There will be someone waiting outside the gates to see you safely away from Otorongo's estate."

"To the river?"

"I make no promises," Thohtzin replied firmly. "Discuss it with your superiors. If you agree, give the hawk's feather you already hold to the guard at the warehouse in an hour's time."

"Agreed," Blake said at once.

He threaded his way back through the thronged streets, waited for another party to enter the show rooms and followed with them. Lo Sige was in charge of the display, and Blake caught his eyes as he moved behind a screen and so into the interior where he sped upstairs to their living quarters.

Marfy, wearing her merchant clothing, sat at the table there, industriously recording, by the New Britain method of a finger-key machine, the data Varlt dictated.

"What happened?" she demanded eagerly when she sighted Blake.

With some editing, omitting the hinted danger to her sister, Blake told them what he had learned from Thohtzin.

"We can get her out easily!" Marfy was out of her seat, her face lighted. "I can call her, she will come. You will not even have to enter that portion of the palace! Oh, this will be easy, Com, it will!"

"You can contact her, let her know that I am coming—"

"That *we* are coming," she corrected Blake sharply.

"That is impossible! Women here do not roam freely, except to travel to the docks for departure—" Blake began.

"Therefore, I shall be another hunter like you. I tell you, Blake Walker, only I can bring Marva out. But—oh! he does not know—" She looked to Varlt.

"She has not been able to reach her sister to any extent," the master wardsman explained. "We suspect that they have been keeping Marva under some type of drug control."

"Then how would your going to Otorongo's be of any aid?" Blake wanted to know.

"Because the closer I am to her, the better chance I have of reaching her. And if I cannot rouse her enough to bring her to the gate, I can guide us directly to her. Do you want to have to search the women's quarters?"

To Blake's dismay Varlt nodded approval. Before he could protest, the master wardsman said, "Lo Sige will go with you. Kragon and Laffy will also follow, under cover. You will be warmed with these." He went to one of the traveling chests in the room, threw up its heavy lid, and then manipulated the underside of that until a panel slid open and Blake saw four hand weapons set into a hollow. In shape they were similar to the regulation needler, but much smaller. Wrapping a cloth about his hand, Varlt freed one from its bed and held it out to Blake.

"A new type of needler, shoots a ray instead of a dart. But it is limited by the fact it can carry only six loads. Hold it in your hand, close your fingers on it."

When Blake curled his fingers about the tiny weapon, he discovered that the originally cool substance of its material warmed. He held it so for a long moment and when he released his grip, he discovered that the silvery sheen of its surface had vanished. It was hardly distinguishable from the flesh holding it.

"Now it is sealed to you. If anyone else touches

it, it will explode. However, remember you have only six charges; it cannot be reloaded."

"Where—" Blake marveled at the weapon he had not known existed.

"These are experimental, the only ones of their kind so far. Rogan supplied them—against orders I might add. And each of them costs a small fortune."

A hand shot past Varlt, grasped the second of the four guns. Marfy's fist was not quite large enough to engulf the weapon completely, but Blake saw it changing color as it adjusted to her and her alone. Varlt moved, but the damage was already done.

"I tell you," she said defiantly, "you cannot get Marva out of there without me."

"Unfortunately," Varlt said coldly, "you are probably right. Your mental tie will help. But remember this, girl, throughout the operation orders will come from Walker; you are to depend upon his judgment or that of Lo Sige. I want your oath on that."

Marfy looked from the master wardsman to Blake and then back again. "To put ties on one going into such action is a dangerous thing, Com Varlt."

"You are under wardsman's discipline now, Marfy. And in this, Walker is your senior. He is expected; therefore he must appear there. Were it possible, I would be in his place. Lo Sige may have to take cover if he is suspected by those who will pass Blake. Thus, Walker leads and you listen to him. Understand?"

She nodded acceptance, though Blake believed she still had reservations. He himself had no liking at all for her company in the face of danger.

The hawk's feather passed them through the warehouse door and Blake breathed a little freer when, in disguise, they were on the street. Kragon and Laffy would use their own methods for following.

Outside, the crowds were thicker, and the three kept close together. There was no transportation to be had; every public conveyance that passed was full. So they walked to the borders of Otorongo's estate.

They found a spot behind a masking growth of brush and Lo Sige set his back against the wall. Blake mounted this human ladder and crouched at the top of the wall to look down into a paradise of flowers, trees, and cunningly devised vistas. He reached down and caught Marfy's hands, drew her and then Lo Sige up beside him. Then the three slid down behind a tangle of flowering vine.

XIII

"BUT WHY would anyone want to destroy all this?"
marveled Marfy as they sought cover among ornamental shrubs, weird rock formations, and
other embellishments of a garden which was a
carefully tended work of art.

"A matter of prestige," returned Lo Sige. "To
allow this to be broken up for the cycle celebra-
tions advances Otorongo to the top listing of those
making grand gestures. He probably thrives on
such attention. What—"

Blake froze. One hand warned the others while
he listened, though he depended more on his
inner alert than his ears. He moved in a leap
which brought him half way around, facing left.
There was time for a snap shot at the furred thun-
derbolt aimed at him from under a trellised vine.
That snarling fury struck full against his body and
sent him sprawling, but the claws did not rip. By
the time they both reached the ground, the jaguar
was a limp weight from under which Blake edged
free. One of his six shots was gone—he must keep
that in mind.

Marfy shivered as she gazed down at the unconscious animal, and then, more fearfully, at the
many hiding places about them that could hide
similar surprises. Lo Sige pulled Blake to his feet.

"Wonder how many of those house cats are
running loose here. Not that we shall take the time
to count—"

"Listen!" Marfy's order was not needed. They

could all hear clearly the throbbing steady beat of drums, coming from the interior of the palace.

Lo Sige pushed ahead. They must still keep to cover, but now they must also make sure that the cover did not shelter more spotted hunters. Another wall of white stone embellished with heavy carving, the top being a conventionalized serpent with scales in heavy relief, now loomed before them.

"This is it. Now to find a gate." Blake put his hands on the surface of the barrier. Right or left? Marfy joined him, her palms also sliding along the stone. Now she turned abruptly to the right. Lo Sige watched her for a moment and then signed to Blake to follow her lead.

They were in a narrow space between the wall which was their guide and another erection of very intricately carved stone that acted as a screen between the garden and the wall. Some of the carving was pierced through so that they caught glimpses of foliage and flowers. Several yards they went before finding the door, or a door, in the wall. It was circular, deeply recessed, the portal closed, with no visible latch on their side.

Marfy turned, stood now with her hands tight against the surface of the closed door. Her eyes were shut. When Blake would have put her aside to try the door, Lo Sige caught his arm and held him back, shaking his head emphatically, as if breaking Marfy's concentration would be grave error.

Blake motioned to the wall, urging that he be given a boost up to look beyond. The other wardsman planted his shoulders as he had before, and Blake, so supported, gripped the deeply graven scales, and pulled himself up to the top. If he was now under observation from the house his dark body against the white stone would provide an excellent target.

Beyond lay a second garden, as elaborate as the first. Two long cages of fine wire mesh enclosed a number of trees and a goodly expanse of space. And within them fluttered and sang a wealth of brightly plumaged birds. But it was the door below which riveted his attention. From all appearances, it was no real door but a sealed exit no longer in use. Moreover, on the inner garden side, a bench had been set within the recess, making it a sheltered resting place for strollers.

A soft hiss brought Blake's attention back to Lo Sige. The other wardsman pointed to Marfy. She no longer stood pressed to the unopenable door but was backing from it step by step. Her right hand had gone to her head, fingertips tight to her forehead. Her eyes were still closed, her whole expression one of deep concentration. However, her left hand moved in slow, almost languid gestures toward the sealed door.

Blake looked into the other garden. There was an open path running between the bird cages; only here by the wall was there any cover. Otorongo might throw open his main garden to be despoiled in a grand gesture, but certainly he would only the more strongly protect the inner apartments of his own household.

Gripping the stone scales, Blake swung over and dropped. They must have very little time left before the crowd stormed in. That throng might afford them cover if they could locate Marva and bring her out of this second garden.

The aviary path led right and left, the bulk of the inner palace to the left. Again—danger!

Blake crouched, his stunner ready. A rustle . . . the creeping of another jaguar? His back was to the chill stone of the wall as he sifted every shadow, every suggestion of hiding place. But padded feet equipped with claws did not now steal upon him. The flicker of movement lay closer to ground level than any of the great cats could flatten its body. Blake saw beads of pitiless reptilian eyes, the lift of a spade-shaped head. And he fired, moved by all the revulsion of his species when faced by a snake.

The head went up and back in a twist, then the coils were still. Blake waited before he dared to inspect his victim more closely. A snake, yes, and probably a deadly one. But banded about its whip-like body immediately below the head was a metal ring from which glittered gem beads as cold as the eyes had been. This snake was no wild creature but one of the recognized inhabitants of the palace.

Another soft hiss. Blake raised his head. Lo Sige lay belly down on the wall above. He made a vigorous gesture towards the palace and his lips shaped words so exaggeratedly that Blake was able to catch the meaning: "Wait . . . watch . . ."

Save for the twittering birds, the garden appeared deserted. Blake could see a terrace across the front of the building, or rather a portion of its length, for trees made a screen in between. No guards stood at the doors, no servants showed; the palace might have been uninhabited.

He became aware of a murmur in the air, a distant hum. The sound must have reached and affected the birds even before he was conscious of it, for they called and some began to flutter about as if disturbed. The crowd, come to pick clean Otorongo's growing treasure, gathered beyond the outer wall.

"Look!" Again that mouthing from Lo Sige.

Movement on the terrace. Someone running down the steps, down the aviary path, running and sobbing.

Blake waited by the bench at the sealed door. A girl burst into the open and came towards him, her eyes wide, yet unseeing. If he had not caught her, she would have gone straight on to slam against the sealed door. And as he held her, she fought him, not as if she knew someone held her, but for her freedom, straining against his strength to reach the door.

It was like trying to control one of the big cats, because, as Blake struggled to hold her, she turned and raked him with her nails in a frenzy beyond any human fighting. Lo Sige leaped down, caught up one end of her cloak and whipped the material about her upper arms, pinning them to her body. And all the time her eyes were wide, unseeing, while tears trickled from them and sobs shook her.

Between them they got her up and over the wall, although Blake thought that any moment her violent struggles would alert any guard Otorongo had stationed nearby. But when they had dropped her onto the other side, she was suddenly quiet. Marfy came running, her hands outstretched, to catch her in close embrace. A second later she backed away from her sister and stared at the girl who subsided limply to the ground. Marfy had a haunted, frightened look in her eyes.

"She . . . she . . ."

Lo Sige caught Marfy by the shoulder, drew her away from her sister.

"Drugs, or some kind of induced block," he said sharply. "Take off her skirt!"

Marva was wearing a long skirt, brightly embroidered. The cloak they had twisted about her was more sober of hue, a dusky violet shade, and its only ornamentation was a band of feather work in blue and gold. Lo Sige caught at the drooping branch of a vine on the screen of carved stone. He tore portions from it. The flowers it supported gave off a heavy scent as he bruised and crushed them.

"Wait!" Blake caught his plan. Now he rounded the screen, reaching for the main roots of the vine Lo Sige had stripped. Recklessly he tore long lianas loose, choosing those with the heaviest burden of flowers, and tossed them over the screen. The natives' love of flowers, their delight in those most highly scented, would prove valuable now.

The clamor beyond the outer gates was a rising fury of sound; now separate shouts and cries could be detected. Then came a vast roar—the gates must have been thrown open! Given time, only a small portion of time, and they might get safely away.

Blake dodged once more behind the screen to aid Lo Sige. Marva, securely wrapped in the violet cloak, still lay unheeding of those about her. Her staring eyes were closed and she might have been asleep. Back and forth around her body Lo Sige

was weaving the mass of flowered vine, while
Marfy ranged at either side, snatching at any
flower she could see, pulling them up roots and
all, weaving her loot into any opening left by Lo
Sige's hasty efforts.

In the end they had a bundle of vegetation
which appeared to be a collection of flowers, most
of them cherished rarities. A sapling thrust
through the vines lengthwise provided handholds, and the men swung the bundle up between
them. The shouting and singing in the garden was
coming nearer. They waited at the edge of the
screen until the first of the flower hunters burst
into view. Men and women both, mainly of the
peasant class, carried baskets or crocks or bowls;
they were after not only the flowers but their
roots. Several men, working together, were more
ambitious; they carried spades and began uproot-
ing small trees and tall shrubs. No, in that company the strangers were not going to be marked.

Marfy had turned her sister's skirt inside out,
thus hiding the rich embroidery. Now she thrust
some bulb flowers into that, fashioning a sack
which she flung over one shoulder, keeping her
back slightly bent under the burden and her face
hidden.

"Time to go!"

Blake did not need Lo Sige's suggestion. He was
already moving out. Around them the workers
were far too intent on their own spoils to really
notice them. One or two glanced up briefly before
returning to their digging.

Slow . . . they must take it slow, no matter how
much they wanted to run for the outer gate. If any
guards lingered there, they must not be given the

chance to wonder how this party had managed to do its looting in so short a time.

They delayed by setting their burden down at intervals. Once or twice they were questioned by some of the other looters, but Lo Sige called out slurred answers, as if they were half drunk, and the questioners shrugged or laughed.

"By the gate!" Marfy caught up with Lo Sige and gave her warning in a low voice.

By the gate indeed! It would seem that Otorongo was tasting a new sensation to the full. He was not only on hand to witness the rape of his famous pleasure grounds, he had also invited guests, or at least most of his household, to join him as spectators. By the main gate through which the looters still came, a platform was erected, with an awning canopy overhead and seats. There were the scarlets of dress uniforms, as well as the bright colors of civilian dress. Servants passed food and drink, and some of Otorongo's guests appeared to be laying wagers. All showed interest in the trickle of looters already leaving, sometimes shouting to them an order to display their finds.

"We cannot—" Marfy began.

"We have to!" Lo Sige replied. "Play tipsy, but not too drunk. And you," he ordered Marfy, "get ahead of us. If there is any trouble, run for it."

Blake picked out the man he believed to be Otorongo. He was tall and lean, wearing a very elaborate shirt which a feather cloak half hid. His boots were latched with a noble's turquoises, and his headdress was an upstanding circlet of feathers of the same hue. He was old-fashioned enough to effect heavy earrings which dragged the lobes of his ears well out of shape.

On his harsh Aztec features was an expression of contemptuous amusement, awakening to animation only now and then when the man on his left made some remark. That one wore the dull black cloak Blake knew was the mark of the priesthood. But he did not have the wild locks of hair, the face burned by fanatic asceticism which had marked the priest of the river holding.

"Now, let us go," Lo Sige said in a low voice.

Blake waited for his private warning. There was no immediate alert. So perhaps they were going to get away with this reckless play after all. He followed Lo Sige's lead in a wavering progress toward the gate. Those on the platform were now occupied with choosing from some trays of fruit and small cakes. Other servants filled any waiting cup.

"Ay-yi-yi-yi," Lo Sige sang. His expression was that of a man enveloped in the bliss of realizing a dream.

Blake dared not attempt song, but with what small skill he possessed, he schooled his mien to match his companion's. And Marfy—Marfy was laughing, patting her improvised bag of flowers and roots.

She was safely by the platform . . . they were almost by . . .

"Ho!" The call was imperative, the words which followed it Blake did not understand.

"Walker," Lo Sige ordered in a low voice, "create a diversion. Quick!"

Blake looked up. One of the army officers was leaning over the rail of the platform beckoning to them imperiously. Behind him was Otorongo, eyes upon them.

Create a diversion? Blake rested the carrying

pole on his left shoulder, steadied by his left hand.
He raised his right now in the salute he had seen
the lower castes use in the city. But from that hand
his stunner fired. By luck, Otorongo had turned to
answer some query of the priest. Now he slumped
forward, caught at the rail of the platform. The
officer, startled, turned just in time to catch him.

"Go!"

They were outside the gate before Blake had
time to think, pushing through the crowd. It
would seem that those wishing to strip the gardens were only admitted by numbers and a second group was about to enter.

Another flower-bearing party was just ahead
and Lo Sige and Blake quickened step to add
themselves to the tail of that procession. Thohtzin
had promised assistance outside the wall. Suddenly, in spite of his distrust of the Imperial officer, Blake wanted very much to sight him. But
they were still marching along behind the other
party, fearfully listening for any sound of pursuit.
Some quick wit on that platform might guess their
connection with Otorongo's collapse if their luck
ran out.

A small van stood in a side street, one of the
closed, shuttered vehicles Blake now knew were
used to transport ladies of noble households. This
one, however, bore no family crest and was
shabby, needing paint and heavily coated with
dust. Its back doors opened and the soldier-
messenger of Thohtzin beckoned to them.

For a moment they hesitated. To accept aid
arranged by the other side might be merely post-
poning disaster for a bit. But to tramp on through
the streets with their very conspicuous burden
was to ask for attention they dared not attract.

They turned, Marfy with them, and laid their vine-wrapped burden inside.

"Where do we go?" Blake asked.

"Where you wish," the man answered. "But in—in! We cannot wait. Too many have seen and of those some will remember. We must now lay a false trail."

Over his shoulder Blake saw Lo Sige nod. The other wardsman was already boosting Marfy in. As Blake entered, the doors were slammed with an emphatic click, and when he set his shoulder against them, he found them secured from without.

"Krogan was out there." Lo Sige's hand fell on Blake's arm, his voice a low whisper. "We shall be traced if they try anything. And he was right about too many people seeing us. If they can baffle the pack of hounds after us, should we protest? Now, let us get the lady out of her wrappings."

In the shuttered interior of the car the scent of flowers was thick, almost stupefying. They tore at the vines and leaves, pulling Marva out of her aromatic cocoon and bracing her up on one of the seats close to the slits which gave a fraction of fresh air. Marfy sat beside her, supporting her sister. Her twin's head lolled on her shoulder much as if Marva had been the target of one of the sunners.

"How is she?" Lo Sige demanded.

Marfy shook her head. "I reached her, enough to bring her to us at the wall. But now—it is as if she has gone away. What have they done to her?"

"Thohtzin said they would drug those who guarded her," Blake supplied. "Maybe she had some, too."

"Keep trying," Lo Sige urged Marfy. "We need

her awake. There may be a need for her to help herself."

"What else would I be doing?" she snapped in return. "Where are they taking us now?"

Blake moved to one of the other seats and knelt there as he leaned against the wall of the van, striving to glimpse what lay outside the narrow window slits. These were almost closed and he could see nothing of any use. They were being driven at a slow pace, at the limited speed necessary on a crowded city thoroughfare. Twice they turned corners and now they were picking up speed. Also, whatever road the vehicle followed was certainly not as smooth as it had been earlier.

"We are not going back into the city." Blake was sure enough of that to voice his belief.

Lo Sige went to the front of the van. In the wall between the interior and the driver's seat was a closed hatch through which the passengers must have given orders. The wardsman tried to push that aside, but it did not move.

A moan drew their attention back to Marva. The sobbing that had shaken her earlier now returned as a gasping, as if she strove to fill laboring lungs with air. Lo Sige came quickly, held her head to the van wall at one of the air slits.

"Marva!" Marfy's hold on her sister tightened. She looked to the wardsmen. "She believes she is dreaming."

"Can you take her under control?"

Blake searched through the debris of roots and vines on the floor and came up with a section of tough root. Using force he pushed it through one of the air slits, pried the shutter back, and then passed his improvised tool to Lo Sige who followed his example on the other side of the van.

Green, the heavy green of solid woodland, slipped past them at a speed which, because of their limited range of vision, gave them little chance to see more. Blake could hardly believe that such a dense forest could exist so close to a city; it was as if they were boring into the wilds.

XIV

"THE HUNTING RANGE . . ." Lo Sige made tentative identification.

"And that is . . ." Blake asked.

"A strip of wild land preserved for cermonial hunting. It was marked on the city maps. But if we are heading into that, we are going directly away from the river—"

"To where?" Marfy looked up from her sister.

"We have yet to find out," Lo Sige replied, a bit absently.

By the swaying and bumping of the car they knew that the road must be rapidly deteriorating. And the green approached the van until they could hear the brushing of branches against its body. Of necessity, their progress had slowed. Finally the van stopped. Blake tapped Lo Sige's shoulder.

"I stun the driver and whoever is with him with this. We take over the van . . . back to the city . . ."

"Possible—" the other wardsman agreed.

"Ahhhh-eeee!" Marva threw herself forward, out of Marfy's grasp, sprawling against the forward seat. At the same instant her sister clapped her hands to her head with a similar cry of protest and pain. And Lo Sige staggered like a man who had been struck from behind. Blake felt that mental blow, too. This was no inept, groping mind exploration such as he had been subjected to while a prisoner at the river lord's holding; it was a practiced probe, aimed at taking over minds with talent and training at Vroom level.

Lo Sige twisted, his face a mask of horror and struggle, his lips flattened against his teeth in a tortured, animal snarl. Only his eyes went to Blake. The younger man's shield held as it always had. But that very protection might warn the one who was losing those bolts that he had here an opponent who could not be controlled.

Inch by inch, unable to resist, Lo Sige was drawn to the rear door of the van. Behind him came Marva, crawling on her hands and knees, still moaning. And then Marfy staggered, keeping her feet with difficulty.

Blake jumped to the left. He could hear a fumbling at the back latch. Whoever was out there would not be prepared for trouble unless he knew of Blake's resistance. The warning—yes, that was rising in him, too—was not yet foretelling instant action.

The van door opened and Lo Sige lurched through, his movements jerky, as if not he but another's will moved his limbs. Marva rolled rather than crawled into the open, and Marfy wavered. Blake kicked at the mass of green stuff on the floor. A hand grasped inward as if to capture someone lying there. Blake fired the sunner and flung himself to the opposite side of the van for a wider range of vision.

The man he had rayed staggered back, tripped over a recumbent figure on the ground and fell. Blake fired again at the other still on his feet. One shot now—just one left! Marfy was armed and so was Lo Sige, but only they could use those weapons.

As his second victim went down, Blake saw Lo Sige and Marfy stoop, still moving in that jerky, mindless way, to raise Marva. Together the three began to stumble off away from the van. Blake edged out cautiously. Two men, Thohtzin's messengers and another, lay unconscious. Trees and shrubs walled in the vehicle and the roughest of tracks marked their back trail. But the three under compulsion were rounding the car, apparently about to vanish into the wilderness ahead.

One Blake might have managed to deter, but three he could not stop by physical means. Manifestly they were being led by mental control to some definite goal. And it could not be too far away, for such control could not operate over a lengthy distance. That meant that whoever exercised it was to be found nearby. And since this was a power out of Vroom, perhaps this was the meeting with the real enemy at long last. Whether he faced a trained adept or not. Blake might be able to use his last shot, providing he could get within firing distance. He fell in behind the staggering trio, alert to every noise, prepared to rely on his personal warning.

The track had been a road to this point. Now it was a path, likely once only a game trail. There had been recent attempts to open it, marked by slashed-back vegetation. But the shadows of twilight were gathering fast and Blake found it increasingly difficult to see ahead. They came out at last on the gravel bed of a summer-shrunken riverlet. The water was a thread in the middle of a wide expanse over which the three from Vroom wavered upstream.

Blake followed after, counterfeiting, now that

he was in the open and might be under observation, the uncertain steps of those he trailed. They rounded a bend in the river and before them the twilight dimness was broken by light, not the bright and honest yellow of a fire nor even the colorful beams of this level's lamps, but a blue glimmer which not only hinted of the alien but carried sinister suggestion.

And now—Blake knew! Before them waited the spider who had woven this web, or at least the greatest menace present. There was an aura of satisfaction, of triumph which Blake could feel as well as if he heard it shouted aloud. Whoever awaited them had no doubts at all concerning his complete victory. But, why had he not realized that, in Blake, he had met a securely blocked mind? Or did he not care, believing that since he controlled three, he did not have to worry about the fourth? That meant that he might have other methods besides mental takeover of coping with potential opponents.

The building they approached was artfully camouflaged. Had it not been for the open windows and the light, Blake would not have marked it; the rough stone of its walls might well have been natural extensions of the river bank, and the brush planted on its low roof carried out the illusion of its being part of the earth.

All three controlled captives made straight for the door which was standing open. Blake dropped behind a waterworn rock. There was nothing he could do to help them by walking straight into a trap. He had only one small advantage, a chance to use effectively the shot still remaining in his stunner. If that mental force could be diverted or broken, even for an instant, he would have Lo Sige's aid also.

In the concealed hut the enemy was very confident. Not for the first time Blake longed for a share of the talents of Vroom. Any one of the wardsmen he knew could have learned the number of occupants inside and so been prepared for action. But if Blake had that power, he would also be subject to mind control; he would now be walking as blindly as the other three into that door.

The blue light appeared to conceal more than reveal. The three were silhouetted against it and then vanished as they entered. They might have pushed through a curtain. Blake waited. If the enemy had expected four to enter, there should follow some move to gather the missing one in.

What he waited for came, a blast of mind-force designed to blind, deafen, completely drive identity out of a man. Blake made his decision in that instant: to allow them to think that they had him.

He staggered out from behind the rock, lurched toward the cabin, trusting his performance was realistic enough to deceive for the few moments it would take him to get within firing distance. He came to the door, the blue light curled about his body as if it were a part of that sucking force.

The light was a fog through which he could catch only mist-blurred glimpses of objects; three shadows, one standing, the other two on the floor. Those were Lo Sige and the girls. But Blake could see no one else.

"On!" The command beat at them all.

Lo Sige stooped, lifted one of the girls with infinite labor. The other crawled ahead on hands and knees, by herself. Blake, striving to see through the confusing mist, followed lest he lose touch.

There! The warning came as sharply as it had back in the garden. Right there! But Blake could see no target. Lo Sige wavered back and forth between him and that unseen focus of force.

A barrier—in it another open door.

The warning was so acute now that Blake threw himself forward, passing beyond the blue mist into natural illumination. He avoided falling over a prone body, caught his balance, and faced the man in a cushioned seat, a man who was staring at him with an expression of complete shock. In that instant Blake fired straight into his face, letting the brain behind it have the full force of the stun-ray.

He heard the clang of metal against metal and then was thrown from his feet. The whole floor under him vibrated. Pushing up again, he could see the stranger. The man was slipping limply down, but one hand lay on an instrument board. That panel—it was familiar—

Blake felt the rack of time-dislocation. They were in an outlaw shuttle! And he had no idea of where they were bound or if they had any true destination at all, since that useless hand on the controls might only have sent them spinning out at random.

"What—"

Blake was making for the control seat, although of what he might do, either to halt their trip or to bring them to any level, he had no idea. It was instinct alone that made him try to do something—anything. He looked back at the sound of the other voice.

Lo Sige must have fallen when they took off. Now he braced himself up by his arms, looking about him as might a man slowly coming out of a nightmare-ridden sleep.

Blake was at the control panel, pulling the unconscious pilot away and rolling his body to the other side of the cabin. This shuttle had few of the fittings usual in those of the wardsmen. He went back to the board. A survey of the dials told him one precious fact: they were on a set course, not roaming wildly across worlds with no hope of lighting. But what course that might be and where it would land them only the man he had stunned could answer.

"Hopping?" Lo Sige had staggered after him. He, too, leaned forward to read the dials. "Hopping," he repeated and then shook his head, not in denial but in an attempt to clear his befogged thinking.

Marfy moaned and sat up, her hands pressed to her head. She retched dryly and shivered. But when she looked around, there was the light of reason in her eyes.

Blake explored the cabin. Although it was bare of the usual equipment, he hoped to find a first-aid kit with the stimulants they needed. And in a cubby he came upon the survival kit which he knew no level-hopper dared be without.

One of the tablets he mouthed himself, the rest he passed to Lo Sige who followed his example. Marfy had a third, but when she would have put one between Marva's lips, Lo Sige shook his head.

"We do not know what drugs she has been given. Better leave her alone and see if she can come out of it naturally." He went to kneel by the stranger, studying the slack face. "No one I know—"

"But I do!" Marfy joined him. "That is Garglos!"

"The Project 'copter pilot?" Blake had to reach back for that memory, it seemed so far in the past. The beginning of this venture was already dimmed by all that had happened since.

"Power to the tenth—he must have that to have been able to take over and hold all three of us," Lo Sige commented. "Why should he be acting as a 'copter pilot on a project?" Then he hastened to answer his own question. "Just a cover, perhaps. But why? Well, he should be able to answer that himself."

"When he comes to," asked Blake, "will you be able to blank against him?"

"Not without some aids we do not possess at present. If and when he recovers consciousness, he will have to be put under again at once!"

"I have used up my stunner charges," Blake announced.

Lo Sige put his hand to the sash belt about his middle, confidently at first, then searching, his fingers running swiftly between the band and his body. He looked up, astonishment more nakedly revealed on his face than Blake had ever seen it.

"Gone!"

"Yours?" Blake asked of Marfy.

Her hand went within the wider sleeve of her shirt.

"Gone!"

"But how?"

"Neat." Lo Sige regarded Garglos bleakly. "We

were without doubt, ordered to disarm ourselves
on the way here, and we did so. We have one
chance unless you can be sure of knocking him
out at once at the first signs of his stirring. That is
to get away from the shuttle the moment we are on
level. I do not know how much range his control
has. Did we come very far from the van?"

"I had no way of measuring it; it seemed a good
distance to me," Blake replied.

"So we cannot risk just guessing. And we *have*
to take him in!"

Lo Sige was overly optimistic, Blake thought,
though he did not say that. There was no reason to
believe that they would have any advantage when
they reached the end of this wild voyage across
time. If they were headed for Vroom, there was an
excellent chance they would open the cabin door
on more trouble than they could hope to handle.

"Are we going to Vroom?" It was Marfy's turn
to inspect the dials.

"I do not think so." Lo Sige sat down crosslegged on the floor of the cabin. "He brought us here
to him. He had a travel code set up and waiting, all
prepared to hop and take us along. But I hardly
think he was bound for Vroom. In the first place,
your father, aware there is probably an outlaw
shuttle in action, will have detectors in use. They
can and will trace any crosstime-hopping near
our own world or on regular lines of travel, and
they will be prepared to counter such action. My
guess is we are now on our way to another hideout, one that the mind behind all this believes is
high security."

"An empty world," Blake said.

"Why?"

"That would be the highest security, would it not? No native population to become involved or suspicious."

"Plausible and probable. But there is more than one 'empty' level. Meanwhile . . ." Lo Sige rose and began searching the clothing of the unconscious Garglos. "No weapons. He was sure, very sure, of himself, it would seem. In fact, there is nothing to give us a clue as to our destination. Marfy, is there any chance now of getting through to your sister? Of picking up some impression? She may have the answer or a portion of it if she went to the New Britain world with Garglos."

"No. It is like trying to patch together many small pieces of something that has been smashed to bits. Will—will she continue to be like this?" Marfy gazed at Lo Sige in entreaty.

There was no ready answer from the wardsman. If he had wanted to give her some soothing denial, he could not. Marfy would have known that for deception. So when he remained silent, she stared beyond him at the bare wall of the shuttle cabin.

"There is this," he said gently a moment or two later, "this present confusion may be born of the drug plus Garglos' control. She may come out of it naturally as one awakes from a fever sleep. Otherwise, back in Vroom they will have the necessary treatment. Only, if the need arises, can you handle her? Use control?"

"I can try." Marfy did not sound very hopeful. Her attention appeared to be turned inward, concerned with her own feelings or her abiding fears for her sister.

Warning signal on the board. Blake swept her down to the floor where he lay between her and the inert Marva, his arms outflung across them both in place of the steadying belts. The dizzy spin of a level breakthrough was, he speedily discovered, far worse in this position then when one occupied the usual seat.

At least they could be sure they were not to emerge in Vroom: the interval between their take-off and arrival was not right. Lo Sige was in the pilot's seat, watching the board. Then Blake's sense of equilibrium could not hold against the dislocation of level arrival, and he had to close his eyes, fight down his illness.

There was a shock which sent a shudder through the cabin. Wherever they now were, they had not arrived in a depot. But there was no movement as there had been in the sabotaged shuttle in the turtle world. Blake swallowed and sat up as Lo Sige snapped on the viewplate.

They looked out into a world of night where moonlight cut in sharp rays. Against a starred sky reared peaks of barren rock. And the limited scope of the screen showed them no more than that.

Marfy stirred, sitting up to brush her tangled hair out of her eyes.

"That—that looks like the Project world," she said slowly.

"Might well be." Lo Sige was out of his seat, making adjustments at the door lock. "No pressure suits needed according to the register, so it is livable. We had better do a little exploring. "You"—he nodded to Blake—"keep watch on him. I do not know how long he will stay unconscious. But I have no wish to march back here under his control."

Against his will, Blake recognized the sense in

that. He watched the wardsman through the lock, and then stripped off his own sash belt, tearing it into strips. He might not be able to put Garglos' mind in bonds, which was what they really needed, but he could see that the ex-pilot was otherwise secured. Hoisting him into the seat, Blake made him fast there with knots over which he spent some time and care.

Marfy continued to watch the scene on the screen. They saw the shadow which was Lo Sige appear at one corner and go off again. The girl broke the silence first.

"Garglos must have been very sure of safety when he brought us here, sure that no one was going to cause him any trouble."

"How long could he hold you under full control?" Blake asked.

"I do not honestly know. He might not have much trouble with Marva as she now is. But Lo Sige and me—together we would not be easy to hold for long."

"Which means he expected help at this end. Someone connected with the Project?" Or, he added silently, a gang of his own out here in the wilderness. Either way Lo Sige, for all his training and ingenuity, might be walking straight into the arms of the enemy. Blake's only assurance was his own absence of inner warning.

He found it hard to keep still; he prowled around the small cabin, making sure every few moments that he checked on Garglos. But to all outward appearance their prisoner was still under the influence of the stunner. Was that a knock at the outer hatch? Lo Sige on his way back or— someone else? Blake crossed to put an ear to the wall . . .

Danger! Then a mind-stab, this time aimed at him and severe enough to make him reel. Hands caught at Blake's feet and ankles, dragging him down. He glimpsed Marva's upturned face, and her dull unfocused eyes. And over her head he saw the tenseness of the bound body in the seat. Garglos had struck. Marfy, too, sprang at Blake, a spitting fury, carrying him all the way down with her weight.

XV

Both girls fought him on the floor, attempting to immobilize him. Garglos had not yet opened his eyes, but the fury of his mind-stab at Blake abated. The ex-pilot could not continue to hold that pitch and still keep the girls in action. This was no time for half measures. Blake strove to free an arm. He must knock Marfy out and quickly. But she was a clawing, raging fury and he had all he could do to protect his eyes from her raking nails. Marva lay across his legs, pinning them tight with her arms, human bonds from which he could not kick free.

The sound of the hatch opening, and a face loomed over Blake: Lo Sige, but the wardsman's face was blank of any intelligence. Blake saw, too, the blow aimed at him, felt sharp pain—then nothing at all.

Blake lay in a drift of rising snow and the chill of it seeped through his body so that his hands and his feet were numb. No, it was not snow and he did not feel a chill. He lay in ashes recently raked from a bed of coals, searing him with their heat. Beyond in a wild whirl danced Marfy and Marva together with Lo Sige, while Com Varlt pounded a huge drum. When they had done, they would take his heart to feed to the great tortoise that brooded on a rock well above the fiery bed on which Blake lay.

Boom—boom—ever the drum and the whirling figures of the dancers. Snow . . . ashes . . . snow . . . Swing through time, crosstime, world after

world, and in none a place for him. So, when he
reached the end of that swing, he would pitch on
out of time forever and be lost in blackness without end. Swing . . . boom . . . swing . . . boom
. . .

Blake thought he cried out then, but there was
no answer to his incoherent appeal for help. The
tortoise head turned and yellow, inhuman eyes
regarded him without pity. Swing . . . boom . . .

The burning was inside him, not without.
Snow—if he could scoop up some of the snow to
put in his mouth. Blake strove to move his hands,
to grasp the wet cool snow. Snow . . . ashes . . .
No, now his hands rasped across a hard, unyielding surface.

No more drumming. He no longer saw anything
save darkness. Then, slowly, he became aware
that that existed under the cover of his own
eyelids. But the burning was still a part of him,
and he made feeble motions, seeking relief. Not
the boom of the drums—no—but sounds—
continuous sounds and with them an urgency
that he did not understand but that made him
restless. At last Blake forced open his eyes.

He looked up at a gray expanse which was not
open sky, for it had corners and was upheld by
walls of the same color. To turn his head cost
effort, but he did it, and discovered he was not
alone. The three who had whirled about him in
frenzied dance lay there as if they had worn out
life itself in their leaping. As he watched, Marfy
moved feebly, rolled her head. Her eyes looked
into his.

"Blake?"

His name was the thinnest of whispers but he

heard it, and, oddly enough, so hearing gave him
a fraction of strength. He stiffened his hands and
arms against the rocks on which he lay, pushed up
into a sitting position.

The sound was a moaning, coming from Marva
and Lo Sige.

"Blake—water—" Marfy's whisper came a little
louder and more demanding.

He looked about the room in which they lay.
The surface of the floor was smoothed rock. But
the walls he had seen before, at least their like, in
the Project camp.

Camp . . . supplies . . . water . . . His thinking was slow and sluggish, but Blake fitted those
three words together making sense. Door . . . out
. . . water . . . Turning his head was a task which
made appalling demands upon his small reserve
of strength. There was a door, or the outline of
one. He could not get to his feet, but he could
crawl—

"Blake?" The whisper was now a low wail.

He paused, turned his head and refused to surrender to the dizziness that movement caused.
His mouth seemed filled with the ash of his de-
lirious dreaming. Somehow he croaked an answer.

"Water . . . go get water . . ."

"Water?" Marfy struggled to her hands and
knees.

Blake resumed his all-fours progress towards
the door. Once there he set his shoulder against it
and put what force he could into an outward
shove. But there was no give. He tried again and
then beat upon it with his fists.

They were shut into this place. There was no

way out! And the thought of water had aroused his thirst fourfold. Water—he must have water!

"No—no—" Marfy joined him. She caught at one of his beating hands, her fingers weakly encircling his wrist. "This way." She flattened his hand against that unyielding surface and moved it, not outward but to the right. This time the door obeyed, sliding into the wall.

They crawled into a corridor. This must be the Project base, but . . . Blake halted to listen. Not a sound, not even the hum of machinery. Down the hall another door stood open and across its threshold lay . . .

"Oh!" Marfy cowered back against Blake, clutching at his shoulder with fingers that dug into his flesh. He freed his arm and pushed her back against the wall.

"Stay here." He had seen death before in many guises and he did not doubt that he saw it again here and now.

It was a long journey down the length of the hall to reach the body. The head was turned from him, resting on an outflung forearm. Blake had to move it to see the face. And it was a face he knew. Sarfinian! Blake had served an apprentice run with the dead man, a wardsman tech responsible for shuttle and communication installations at the depots.

Blake glanced beyond the body into the room it guarded. Equipment, mostly for communication, now a mass of wreckage—deliberately done. Much of the wiring fused, delicate installations broken. Someone had made very sure that no one would again send a message from this point!

He edged to the wall, used it as a support to get

to his feet. Then, leaning heavily against it, he staggered back to where Marfy crouched.

"Who?" she asked him as he reached down to try and draw her up beside him.

"A wardsman—a com tech. Do you know, is this the Project?"

"Yes!" She was still straining to look past him at the body.

"Where . . . supplies?" It was such an effort to keep his feet and hold the girl against him that Blake had little energy left for words.

Marfy turned her head slowly, looking up and down the corridor. "There"—she pointed to the opposite end—"think . . . through there . . ."

"Stay." For the second time Blake gave that order. It would be all he could do to get himself going; he could not support her, too. But when he lurched along against the wall, she followed, and he did not waste breath protesting.

Somehow he made it to the end of the hall where there was a larger room. And this one he recognized; it was the dining place where he had once made an uncomfortable meal under Kutur's eyes. There was a muddle of dishes on the table and close to him a half-filled cup of liquid.

Never had he tasted anything so good as that cold and bitter brew. He swallowed half of it in a gulp and nursed the rest. The sound of Marfy's stumbling progress was louder. Blake turned, holding on to the table as she crept into the room. Then he offered her the cup. She had slumped to the floor, sitting there with her back against the wall. Taking the cup with both her shaking hands, she got it to her mouth.

"More? For Marva . . . Lo Sige . . . more?"

Blake made a cautious circuit of the table, peering into the cups. Two of them did hold more than just dregs and he poured that bounty together. The plates had only dried remnants of food. But somewhere beyond must be the kitchen unit with more supplies. Blake carried the second cup to Marfy.

"Where is the supply room?"

"Kitchen unit through there." She tried to stop the shaking of her hands by pressing the cup hard against her.

Blake followed her directions. The kitchen unit was an efficiency one. One fed the packaged supplies into the proper slots, watched them emerge ready for consumption on use-trays and plates. But the cupboard above the preparation unit was open, its shelves bare; none of the raw materials remained.

And that was the way it was, he knew bleakly some time later. Water, yes, they had water. With a river of it outside, those who had abandoned them had seen no reason to deny them water. But food—there was no food. Just as there was no usable form of communication, nor shuttle, nor any sign of recent occupancy except the dead man guarding the wreckage.

Lo Sige now occupied the seat which once Kutur had filled. Marva, her hands and sometimes her body trembling beyond her power to control, was still given to short periods of blankness but at other times was almost restored to their world. Marfy and Blake shared the table that was bare of all they needed to restore them.

"This is it." The senior wardsman stared down at three small packets. Not food but sustain tablets, found after an agonizing search of the private quarters, each of which had the signs of hurried evacuation. Sustain tablets were not food. The energy they supplied would be false, burning out the user when there was no proper nourishment to take with them.

"The com?" Marva was in one of her alert periods. "Can we not repair the com?"

"You saw what had been done to it," Marfy reminded her gently.

"But we cannot just sit here and—and—"

"No. It is in our breed to keep on struggling," Lo Sige said. "But the com is useless."

Blake looked up. "You have an idea?" Almost his question seemed an accusation.

The other shrugged. "It is so wild a chance that we dare not pin any hope at all on its succeeding."

"But there is a chance," Marfy caught him up. "If there is any thing we can do?"

"Like what?" Blake strove to bring them back to cold reality.

"Perhaps it may be only supposition, but—" Lo Sige broke off abruptly and then added, "I do not think that there will be any search parties sent to hunt us. After what was done here, those responsible will try in every way to erase this base. However, though, they have destroyed the com, they have not destroyed the depot terminal."

"And what good is that without a shuttle?" Blake wanted to know.

"You mean—the thin wall of time?" Marfy stared at Lo Sige. "But—but that is only a superstition, is it not?" Her question carried a pleading to be denied.

"We have always considered it so," Lo Sige

agreed. "But this is a time when we must seriously test that superstition."

The "thin wall of time"? Blake had a faint memory of those words—or others like them. A discussion . . . when . . . where . . . with whom? He could not remember now. His mind was still sluggish. But he could pick out of that hazy recall some facts. No, not facts, just surmises and guesses.

The depots of the crosstime ventures were regularly established points and many of them had been maintained in constant operation for generations. There was speculation that at such depots there was a kind of thinning of the barrier of time, that constant travel from level to level caused weak points. So far the theory was supposition only, the experimentation needed to prove or disprove it too much of a risk to the whole system to be allowed.

"But this Project has not been established very long," Blake objected. "The thinning must have time to work—if it does. There needs to be a long period of constant travel."

"That is only another supposition," Lo Sige replied. "And been established for some eighteen months. There has been fairly frequent contact: check visits, shipping in and out of personnel, supply trains making regular calls. It may not have had the heavy use of such depots as Argos or Kalabria, but it has had many visits."

"What can we do?" Blake had guessed at the other's purpose: to give the girls something to think about, to revive a thread of hope to keep them from going over the edge of sanity when the full despair of their situation struck. How long *could* one live without food? Longer than without water, he knew.

"We'll hunt in the com room for materials to build an amplifier." Lo Sige opened one package of sustain tablets. "One each of these." He spilled out the small pills.

"Amplifier for what?" Blake was willing to go along with the other's elaborate pretense, but he could not help asking questions.

"For our signal. Linked, and with an amplifier . . ." Lo Sige looked to Marfy and her sister.

"Do—do you really think we can do it?" Marfy responded.

"Anything is worth a try, is it not?" Lo Sige swallowed his tablet. "You have one strong point of reception: Erc Rogan. His mind is tuned to yours; he must be hunting you. So he will be in excellent receptive state."

"You mean," Blake tried to keep his instant incredulity out of his voice, "that you are going to try to think yourself out?" Insane! Surely Lo Sige did not mean that. And if the girls accepted his suggestion seriously, then he, Blake Walker, was the only one still mentally stable. Their experience under control by Garglos? Had that, could that, do this to a wardsman like Lo Sige? If Blake had been asked to list those among the corps whom he knew would be the last to crack under pressure, he would have chosen this man first. That might only prove that he was a bad judge of character. But then he had no idea how deeply the stress of mental take-over could penetrate, since he had never had his own natural protective barrier forced.

"You might term it that," the other continued,

"loosely." He was smiling a little. "With an amplifier we might reach someone who was attuned closely to one of us—"

"Father!" Marva broke in. Again there was a flicker of intelligence in her face.

"But if a shuttle call only reaches for a few levels . . ." Blake began and then stopped. If this was a game for the benefit of the girls, why wreck it by argument? Let them go on believing as long as they could. "You know more about it than I do." He tried to make his tone hearty, as if he did accept such lunacy as fact. "I am the deaf and dumb man in this field, remember?"

Marfy smiled at him. "Do not underrate yourself."

"I am not likely to," he replied as he swallowed his tablet ration.

They faced the disaster that was the com room after they had carried the body of the wardsman into the quarters which had once been Kutur's and sealed the door. Blake ripped, unscrewed, sorted, under Lo Sige's direction, while the senior wardsman dealt in other ways with the spoil. At intervals Marfy aided first one and then the other. Marva spent most of the time stretched on coverings taken from the bunks and piled in a heap in the corridor. They all wanted to stay together, as if something lurked within the empty shell of the Project Headquarters which was only kept at bay by their remaining in company.

Twice Blake went to the river for water. The pens built by the Project showed the scars of the storm that had broken them during his first visit. Only one had been repaired, the machinery to deal with the others standing derelict in the open.

They had to rest often. Their energy came only

from the tablets. The dull cramps of hunger, their weak and shaking hands, were ever-present warnings that their labors could continue only for a short time longer.

Day became night again. They crawled into the corridor, huddled on the bedding, and rested. Blake was not sure he slept. He thought that he must be having increasing periods of blackout. Once he awakened to find himself squatting on the floor of the com room, striving to free bits of unmelted wire from a slagged mass.

It was again day, maybe the next or another even later, when Lo Sige led a halting procession into the room that had been the terminal for the shuttles. Blake subsided against the wall, watching groggily as the other wardsman, working with infinite slowness and the utmost care, set down the weird contraption on which they had labored for so long, making sure of its position by much checking.

Lo Sige was determined to carry the farce clear through to the end, Blake thought dully. They would remain here from now on, getting weaker, at last sliding into unconsciousness and the final end. Perhaps never to be found. They had no way of knowing what was happening along the crosstime routes. And they would probably never know the real reason that lay behind all that had happened to them.

"It is right?" Marfy's eyes were huge. The stain and paint used in her disguise had faded, and her face was very thin and drawn.

Lo Sige raised himself from a last check that had necessitated his lying flat before the patchwork machine.

"As far as I can tell."

"Now?" She made the single word a question.

He took the remaining packet of tablets from his belt, opened it to let the white rounds roll out on his hand. Marfy crossed the room and came back, supporting her twin against her.

"Father," she was saying clearly into Marva's ear as they came. "Think of Father. Make a mind picture of him. Call . . ."

Her sister nodded. "Yes, I know."

Lo Sige handed each of the girls one of the pellets, held another toward Blake.

The latter shook his head. "You need them more." He did not, could not, believed that what they were going to try would save them. He was content to wait out the end without any more stimulants.

The three others sat by the machine now, linked hand in hand. Maybe they would be content, even happy, in their belief that they *were* doing something, making a concrete effort for survival. Blake was too tired to care any longer; he did not even envy them their capacity for hope.

Perhaps he dozed. Time, as it existed here, had no meaning. Blake only knew that whenever he opened his eyes, they were always there, heads sinking forward on their chests. And slowly he came to believe that they were already gone, that only their discarded bodies were still present.

It was raining again. The battering of a heavy fall of water pounded on the roof. How long would it take such storms to demolish the deserted camp eventually and bury five bodies in the ruins? Water . . .

There was a shimmer in the center of the room—the roof must already be leaking. Some spark deep within Blake struggled to move him, to make him call a warning to the others. But it did not matter, they were gone . . .

A shimmer?

NO!

Light hurt his eyes; he had to close them. Then—he looked again—a solid, gleaming surface where nothing had been a moment earlier. This was hallucination, he repeated to himself, even when he saw a hatch opening.

XVI

BLAKE SIPPED from the container held by both shaking hands to his parched mouth. Hallucination? Somehow his thoughts clung to that explanation of his present surroundings. Yet, for a dream, this had a reality he had never known such illusions to hold before, beginning with the taste of food in his mouth, progressing to the fact that he appeared to be seated within a shuttle, a standard two-man model used by the corps.

"That is about it, sir. Depots are being shut down all along the line on orders from Vroom." Blake heard the pilot's voice droning on over his head. "The wind-up signal is out—for what that is worth under the circumstances."

"Wind-up?" Lo Sige's voice, thin and drained, came from the other side of the cabin. "What—what does that mean?"

"To'Kekrops!" The anger in the ready answer was hot. "He forced across a Question in Council, carried it by a majority of two. Erc Rogan was not there, nor many of the others. The rumor is that opposition members were not all notified in time."

"Even so, how could he move so promptly?" Lo Sige sounded baffled.

"Oh, apparently he had been planning his coup for a long time. Squads of specially enlisted temporary wardsmen came through to the main depots and assumed control. There was trouble at at least two, but our men didn't have a chance. We never kept large crews anywhere along the line.

They threatened to maroon anyone who did not surrender quietly, just as they treated your party. And I think that happened elsewhere. We have no real news, mostly just rumor. The message lines are all in their hands and all that is being broadcast is the order to come in at once and make no trouble."

"So you are on your way to Vroom?"

Blake, with food inside him, now paid closer attention to the conversation. The man in the pilot's seat was unknown to him. He had rugged features, and a small white sunburst of an old scar on one temple. His duty coveralls bore a narrow piping of green, the mark of a level explorer. And noting that, Blake was not surprised at the hesitant answer the stranger now made.

"I can run you to Vroom if that is where you really want to go."

"But you were not bound there?"

"Every shuttle reaching Vroom is impounded—that one piece of information has come down the line—and our men are taken into custody as they return. No, I was not on my way to Vroom."

"To a hideout?"

The stranger's lean hand rubbed along his chin line. "I am on exploration service, sir. Being marooned without resources on a successor world is one thing; having a base of one's own to return to is another."

"I take it you are not alone in your reaction?"

The other turned his head, looked at Blake who met his glance steadily, at the two girls, wrapped in coverings on the floor, who appeared to be asleep.

"No, I am not alone. There are others."

"And among them perhaps—Eric Rogan?"

"Yes. But just now he is in no condition to go on even if he wished. He was at the Saracossis Depot when they tried to take it over by force. We are certain they had orders to make sure of Rogan. He was rayed but made it out on a flash hop. They are using top-power mind control, and he is afraid they will make him into a puppet to mouth To'Kekrops' rot."

"Then we are not heading for Vroom. Will you take us to your hideout?"

"What about them?" The wardsman gestured o the girls. "They need medical attention. We have very little."

"They are Rogan's daughters; they can be used also. They would not choose to be in Limiters' hands."

"All right, if we can still make it. They have been slapping automatic recalls on shuttles, that was the last warning through. Unless it was just a threat . . ."

"Automatic recall? They don't care what happens to a crew, do they?" There was a savage bite in Lo Sige's demand. "In order to be safe from that you would have to disconnect part of the code director."

The other shrugged. "Which might dump you anywhere in any world, yes. But I am ready to take that chance. None of us fancies being marooned; only some things might be even worse."

"What about this hideout of yours? Coded, of course?"

The big man grinned. "That it is not! I have been on lone probe for five years now; my rank entitled me to a choice and I took it. The only record that will show up under the name of Faver Teborun, if they do any delving into assignments, is the waiver I made in order to get free rein. I have an uncounted base in the middle of Radiation Two belt."

Radiation Two belt: a series of worlds—how many no one was yet sure—where the past atomic holocaust had sent several time lines into oblivion as far as the human race was concerned. To go exploring there had taken nerve or the kind of recklessness that was thought to be beyond a qualified wardsman.

Teborun continued to smile. "It is uncoded, a wild place. Some radiation, of course, but it was not totally burned off. It's rather like Vroom. And there are a lot of queer mutations but none remotely human. At least none I have seen. It is a pocket where tracers are not likely to drop off for a look. I made two reports about it, both directly to Erc Rogan and not recorded on regular tapes. As far as the records show, I have been worlds away, doing some trading on the Icelandic-Vineland level."

"How many of our men reached it?"

"Don't know. Rogan got in with four and set up a limited call—one to New Britain and a couple more—for men he hoped to recruit before they were netted. There were about a dozen when I left just after your message got through. Say, how did you do that, anyway? The com was dead from E1045 back."

"We tried another method." Lo Sige did not elaborate. "Something new."

"Something we can use to draw in some of the

other boys?" Teborun pressed. "No use letting goodmen walk into Limiter traps or take what they tried to give to Rogan."

"It was an experiment. I do not know whether it would work again."

Somewhat to Blake's surprise, Teborun did not push for any more details. And shortly thereafter the warning of level breakthrough came. Blake lay flat on the floor, close beside the girls, as the vibration shook them.

They looked through the hatch of the shuttle into what was indeed a strange place, the center of what might have been a gigantic stone globe. Well overhead was a break in its surface through which they could see the blue of what appeared to be normal sky.

The walls, sloping up and inward, were smooth as if they had been worked upon by human hands for a long time. Yet there was an alien air to the place which did not match the work of men at all.

Blake stumbled out of the hatch into a small crowd of men, some of them wearing the coveralls of wardsmen, still others a variety of strange dress as if the wearers had been hastily snatched from a number of different successor worlds. Pushed to the side of the globe, well away from the area the shuttle now occupied, were four or five more of the traveling machines. It was a rendezvous of refugees and fugitives.

"Rogan? Where is Rogan?" Lo Sige asked. "We have his daughters."

He was faced, as was Blake, with raised weapons, with closed, hostile faces. Only when Teborun dropped out of the hatch did the hostility lighten.

"What is the matter here?" demanded the probe scout.

He was shoved to one side by an armed man who looked into the cabin and then called over his shoulder, "It is the truth this time. They have a couple of women with them."

Teborun caught the man's arm and whirled him back against the wall of the shuttle. "All right, now suppose you begin to make some sense! You know why I went out—because Erc Rogan asked me to. And now I am back with his girls, plus a couple of our men who were marooned with them. Why the stunners? Where is Rogan? And just what has been going on here?"

There was a clamor of replies which was finally reduced to a disturbing story. Shortly before their own shuttle had arrived, another had appeared. The pilot had called from the hatch for Rogan, saying his daughters were on board, badly injured. The fact that Teborun was not in sight aroused suspicion in some of the men. Two had crowded into the cabin, in spite of the pilot's attempt to bar them. There had been sounds of a commotion inside and the shuttle had taken off. The trap had failed, but it *had* been a trap.

And the knowledge that the enemy had known just where to find them was unnerving. Events were moving so fast that the fugitives were unable to adjust to the shifting sands under them. Instead of the firm base they had known all their lives, the security of the corps, they were faced with utter chaos. The realization that they were hunted, that they might be marooned in some alien world, gnawed at their ability to think clearly.

There had never been a period when crosstiming was free from risk, and those risks these men had accepted without question for years. But those had been familiar risks, not engineered by their own people. Now return to home base was denied them if they would keep their freedom; they could not depend upon the loyalty of their own people, and certainly not upon the authorities. And they might not even be able to count on their shuttles should they be put on automatic recall.

Blake and Lo Sige sat on stools by the couch on which Rogan rested. His left leg was bandaged, his face worn with tension and pain. He looked years older than the man who had selected Blake as one of the team pledged to find Marva. That daughter and her sister now lay in an adjoining cave, one of those which led out of the sphere Teborun had chosen for his depot. Marfy had recovered to the point of talking with her father, but Marva was deep in a stupor.

"The Limiters having located this level," Rogan spoke with his normal rush of words, "they will be back, never doubt that. And what good are our few weapons against their mind control?"

"How did it all happen, sir?" Lo Sige asked. "Oh, we knew that the Limiters were trying to make trouble. But this—it blew up so suddenly!"

Rogan's mouth twisted. "We made the unforgivable mistake: we underestimated To'Kekrops! Vroom has come to depend upon crosstiming for most of the materials of life. We draw raw materials, food, the necessities of life as well as luxuries, from the successor worlds. For hundreds of years we have expanded and established depots, drawn energy from sister worlds. The Great War left us a handful of mutant survivors in a world three-quarters forbidden to human life. Only crosstiming saved us from total extinction.

"Thus, the man or men who control crosstiming also control Vroom as surely as if they hold each and every one of us here." Rogan raised his hand palm up and slowly curled his fingers inward. "To prevent any dictatorship we thought we had taken every precaution. The Hundred were selected with utmost care, the corps was sifted and sifted. But people forget when the good times go on and on. When there are no visible alarms nor enemies, swords rust, shields catch cobwebs in dark corners. I believe I can say, and be right, that the people of Vroom—except for the few who carry on the labor—do not realize just how much our world is supported by successor worlds they may never have heard of. There has always been a fanatic element among us. In the past, such people were rendered harmless by the disinterest of the rest; they were mainly talkers who feared contact with other levels. There have been wild rumors of disease, of possible importation of deadly weapons—as if any of the worlds have any worse than those we once turned upon ourselves—of ideas from abroad.

"When a people grows fat and indolent, rumors and such tales add spice to life. They are repeated as idle gossip, then they begin to be believed. A well-published disaster that affects persons from Vroom is caught up, magnified, used by shrewd troublemakers. For the past few years there has been a growing feeling that all crosstiming is dangerous.

"The reports of the corps are closed to the general public. A family from Vroom may visit the Forest Level or one of the other three approved holiday places. For the rest, they have only hearsay to depend on. And the worst is always more quickly believed and relayed than the good.

"A close-down of the corps might, in itself, accomplish two things to To'Kekrops' liking. First, it will feed the belief that danger exists crosstime to the extent that even trained men dare not risk such contact. Secondly, it will bring a pinch in our economy that will be felt by all, including those who have had no opinion concerning crosstime one way or another. Then the formation of a second corps could begin. And that corps will be, naturally, under Limiter command.

"Levels could then be looted openly under a freebooting raid system. Some of the loot, dumped in Vroom, could win To'Kekrops more and more adherents among those who have felt the pinch and would react to the plenty. Our own men, under mind control, may—probably already have—parrot what he would have them say. A few men in key positions, under his influence or direct mental control, must have begun this takeover, and the poison will spread rapidly because it comes from within corps ranks."

"But the situation cannot be hopeless." Lo Sige leaned back against the wall. "Something built with care for centuries can not just collapse overnight!"

"Disorganization at the center can work great havoc," Rogan replied. "Take a city . . . say, on your home world, Walker. What would happen if the lighting system failed, and with it the water supply, the heating, the communications? All gone in a day or part of a day. What would the result be?"

"Murder, literally murder!" Blake replied. "The city would die." He remembered a city on another level close to his own where death had come in a war it was not prepared to resist. "But afterward . . . there might be survivors maybe one man or several who could lead the survivors and make them want to try again. But they would not have what they had before, and it would take years to gain any kind of order."

"Years we do not have!" snapped Lo Sige.

"No, years we do not have," Rogan assented. "However, we have really only one enemy, a spider at the center of the web. Bring down To'Kekrops now, before he becomes too deeply entrenched, and swift disaster can recoil upon all his party. He is not the man to delegate authority—his type never does. We have to get at him."

"And he is in Vroom, protected undoubtedly by the best guard ever assembled since the Great War," commented Lo Sige dryly.

"Just so. We are not equipped to fight war up and down crosstime," Rogan pointed out. "We have few men, practically no supplies. We can accept marooning and save our skins, or we can try to get To'Kekrops."

"He will have mind control ready to take over anyone who sets foot on Vroom. Do you have any defense against that, sir?" asked Blake.

"I have one block—my own. Since the first reports of unrest, I have worn it. That is why he failed to pick me up."

"One man can be stunned or overpowered physically," Lo Sige pointed out, "or even rayed and removed permanently."

"I am too good a tool to kill off, at least immediately," Rogan said simply. "Mind-controlled and speaking for him, I would be worth more than he would want to throw away. Yes, they would try to take me alive. Then, stripped of my block . . ." He spread his hands in a gesture of defeat.

Rogan was talking around some idea, Blake knew, and he thought he could guess what that was. Blake Walker, alone of the men in this temporary refuge, did not have to depend on any mechanical block, could not be taken over by the Limiters' mental storm troopers. But the Limiters must already know that if Garglos had reported in as he surely must have.

"They saw you only as you were in the New Britain disguise." Though Blake knew that Lo Sige could not have read his thoughts, yet the other spoke as if he had done just that. "In Vroom you are relatively unknown. Oh, To'Kekrops will have heard of you as having been with Marfy Rogan. Whether his information goes much further—"

"It should, if he is as good as you think." Blake was emphatic.

Rogan might have been pursuing his own thoughts as they spoke, and not hearing a word, for now he broke in. "I am the only bait he will rise to, the only one who can get To'Kekrops."

"And you have not the least chance of reaching him uncontrolled." Lo Sige spoke with authority.

"But I have!" What made him say that? Blake

wondered. What wild idea . . . ?

Both men were watching him now with a curious intentness as if they could will from him the answer they needed.

"You say he knows I was with Marfy. He must also know how we were marooned at the Project. Can it be possible that only because he was sure of our whereabouts he dared to try to trap you, sir? He could not have foreseen our escape."

"He now has the two men taken from here in his trap. He'll question them," Rogan said.

"Yes, but they were taken before we arrived. They know you sent for your daughters; they do not know whether we ever came. You could not be sure of our safety yourself then."

"True. And no one understood how I knew where to send for you." Rogan hitched himself up on his bed.

"What do you have in mind, Walker?" the wardsman asked.

"I imagine that when they discovered I was with Marfy on that sabotaged trip, the Limiters would have had me investigated as a matter of course."

Both men nodded agreement to that.

"Then To'Kekrops must know I am not a native of Vroom. Therefore, I represent a factor of which he cannot be sure. Would he not accept the idea that I am what is called a 'soldier of fortune' in my world, a mercenary willing to change sides for gain? I might say I was impressed into the corps because they could not erase my memory. And this is true in one way. If I approached him and offered a deal . . ."

"You would be willing to attempt this?" Rogan was still watching him closely.

"I take it that supplies here are low," Blake counterquestioned. "How long are we prepared to sit out a search? And now they must have a code for this world. You may scatter and hide, but eventually the advantage is all theirs. Our small advantage is to move first."

"If the eventual advantage rests with them, why would To'Kekrops be ready to make any deal with you?" cut in Lo Sige.

"I think he wants quick results. Could he comb the whole of this level if you went into hiding? And you have shuttles. What is to prevent your hopping? Teborun is an experienced probe explorer; he could even find you another uncoded world."

"Good arguments. But To'Kekrops is no fool."

"You mean I'm no match for him? I do not pretend to be. But if he judges my motives by . . ."

"Those most familiar to him?" Rogan nodded. "Yes, he could believe in you. And he could not have you mind-read to reveal anything else!"

"Getting to To'Kekrops is only the beginning," Lo Sige said. "What then?"

"Does he hate you enough, sir," Blake asked Rogan, "to make this a personal duel?"

Rogan twisted at the blanket covering his legs. "Of that . . . no, I am not sure."

"At least he would send a party in for you, and with me as guide. And you can lay a trap here. That would be up to you."

Lo Sige smiled faintly. "We are reduced to the thinnest of chances. Let us hope that fortune has no quarrel with us from now on!"

XVII

STRIPPED OF BOTH disguises he had worn, that of the New Britain trader and the frontier hunter of the Empire, and clad once again in service coveralls, Blake settled himself alone as the pilot of a shuttle. What had led him to make the reckless offer that had brought him here he was not sure. But he was not one to wait for any fight to come to him, that he knew. In the past waiting had always been the hardest part of discipline for him. And what he held now as a weapon was not a stunner keyed to his person, but all the information concerning his opponent that Rogan could supply: a list of those who might be of some aid—always providing they were not already under Limiter control—and a menal map of crosstime headquarters.

As soon as his machine left on the Vroom flight, the majority of the refugees would take to the outer world on that level, hiding out from a return raid. And Lo Sige would begin to set up the trap against Blake's return with Limiter forces.

Teborun had coded to run to Vroom; Blake had no fears of not arriving there safely. And once into the corps terminal, the rest would be improvision on his part. He was no hero; he was merely the only man naturally equipped to fill this present role.

The return was like any normal trip. But when the signal told him Vroom was outside, Blake sat quietly facing the controls for a moment or two. He did not doubt that To'Kekrops would be interested in him; he had only to work on that interest strongly enough to get a personal interview. And then work again, this time on the animosity between the Limiter leader and Rogan, and talk better, more persuasively then he ever had before. And maybe, if such talk did not convince, he might have to make sure of To'Kekrops somehow himself. That thought had been in the back of his mind from the first. The Limiters must be brought down! What if they did turn to level-raiding, the worst piracy the successor worlds would ever know: snatch, kill, be gone where no other level's law could follow.

Blake stood up. Better leave now or any reception committee out there would begin to suspect. He thumbed the hatch catch, stepped onto the pavement of the terminal. There he fronted rows of shuttles, more than he had ever seen gathered in one space before, not only small patrol ships such as he had just quitted, but also heavier trade carriers fitted for the moving of cargo.

Drawn up before the array of hastily parked shuttles were three men. Two were in the field dress of the corps, but Blake did not know them. The third wore civilian clothing with a wide white band conspicuous on his right sleeve.

It was the latter who aimed a mind probe at Blake.

"You will not get far with that," Blake remarked with a calculated insolence. "I am no meat for your broiling, friend."

The other's concentrated stare broke and then intensified again with a bolt of mind force that hurt Blake but did not crack his block.

The two who flanked the civilian now moved in, their faces expressionless, in their hands one of the few weapons legal on Vroom: stunners. Blake had no desire to be even momentarily subjected to darts from them, even though they had little lasting effect.

"I came through by myself. I am making you no trouble," he said. "Ask To'Kekrops if he wants to see Blake Walker. I think you will discover that any interference with me will not be welcome."

The wardsman to his left had his stunner aimed. He fired in the same instant that Blake read a dawning uncertainty in the civilian's expression. But it was too late. There was a prick at Blake's throat just above the collar line. He slumped forward; he had no defense against this kind of attack.

He awoke to the stinging slaps across his face to discover that, held upright between two men, he was being dragged back and forth while the third slapped him from time to time as a rough but effective way of bringing him back to consciousness. None of his present captors were those who had greeted him in the terminal, and he was now in an office which he recognized as being that of one of the commanders of a sector.

"Get him going." The order, marked by a note of irritation, came from behind. Then those who had supported his wavering walk turned Blake around and headed him toward the desk. He who sat there was Commander To'Frang, a credited officer of the corps. For one or two fuzzy moments Blake puzzled over that. Had the Limiters' takeover failed? Was he now in the hands of those who supported the old regime? Perhaps To'Kekrops' sweep had not been as complete as the men in the field had believed.

Yet Blake was aware not only of the actions of

those striving to arouse him, but also of his warning. And on that he relied more than anything
else. Danger! He could almost sniff it in this room.

"What . . ." Might as well let them know that
he was conscious. But his voice sounded oddly in
his own ears, thin and far away.

The man in the wardsman's uniform, who had
just drawn back his hand for anther slap, changed
his aim and caught a handful of Blake's hair, jerking up his head.

"He is around now," he reported to To'Frang.

"About time. Bring him here."

They dragged Blake to the front of the desk. No
lights reporting movements in the field played
along the controls on its surface. There was only a
line of dull green straight down, signaling returned shuttles. It was something Blake had never
seen before.

But the question To'Frang shot at him now was
not the one he had been expecting at all.

"Where is Com Varlt?"

"Varlt?" Blake repeated. It was hard, coming
out of a stunner-induced daze as he now was, to
adjust to the meaning of that demand. What had
Com Varlt to do with his mission here?

"Varlt!" To'Frang's hands, resting on the desk
surface as if he still wished to press controls and
monitor reports, their fingers crooked, raised as if
to claw the answer he wanted out of Blake.

"You left here with Varlt on a special mission
not recorded. Now where is Varlt?"

"I don't know," Blake answered with the exact
truth. The last time he had seen the master
wardsman had been in the Merchant's house in
Xomatl. There was a good chance that he had been
marooned on that successor world.

"You do not understand." To'Frang schooled both his impatience and his tone. "We have to have Varlt. We cannot organize anything effective against these madmen without leaders such as Varlt."

"I don't know where he is—" Blake had just begun when the Commander's impatience broke its bounds. He got to his feet, leaned across the desk and gripped the front of Blake's coverall, shaking him savagely.

"We got you out of the hands of To'Kekrops' men; we can dump you right back into them, Walker! You are only important because you can lead us to Varlt and for no other reason. We are holding on here by our fingernails. Most of the senior men are now mind-controlled, shouting out Limiter poison on cue. We are trying to get in touch with those still in the field. If we can round up enough and bring them in, we may have a slim chance. Now—where is Varlt?"

"I don't know," Blake repeated for the third time. "We separated in the field. I had to level-hop. And I don't know what happened to him after that."

To'Frang released his hold on Blake, sank back in his seat. Perhaps every word the Commander had said was true. But the alert within Blake warned to walk with care, very great care. And his mission lay elsewhere. He was well recovered from the stunner-induced fog now. If To'Frang and those with him were not cooperating with the Limiters, then how was it that Blake now stood before the Commander's own desk in his assigned office? Business as usual? With crosstiming closed down and To'Kekrops' men waiting in the terminal to snag all arrivals? Hardly!

The Commander nodded, as if Blake's last answer made sense. "Clever, Walker. Play it smart. Only"—his expression now was one of a man deciding to speak frankly—"time is against us. We have been playing hide-and-seek through this building for hours. I had to get here," he slipped his hand along the surface of the desk almost caressingly, "or I had no way to recall the men still out there. The Limiters believe they have marooned them." He grimaced. "But they do not have all lines cut. Not yet. And if we can bring back men such as Varlt, then we have a chance, thin but still a chance. We need that chance, Walker. Where did you leave Varlt?"

"Well away from the local depot." Blake was willing to admit that much. "And I do not see how he could possibly have reached that before it was closed down."

"I do not associate the name Com Varlt with the word impossible." To'Frang smiled faintly. "You went to New Britain. That is one of the marooned levels; they were awaiting the return of their normal three-day shuttle and it was not dispatched. But perhaps we can send it."

"But if Limiters hold the terminal and snap mind-control on each man who comes in, then—"

"How do we plan to take over long enough to land our men? We are working on that now, Walker. And by the way, if you were level-hopping, from just which world did you come?"

"That of Kutur's Project."

"But . . ." the Commander betrayed surprise, "but Kutur has been unmasked as one of To'Kekrops' supporters. How did he—"

"Let me get away? I reached there after he left.

There were indications that there had been trouble—the com had been destroyed and I could get no answers via emergency—so I came through."

Would the Commander buy that?

"And what have you to say that is so important for To'Kekrops to hear?" To'Frang pounced like a cat with prey well within paw reach. Blake did not have to act his surprise and the Commander laughed softly.

"We had eyes and ears in the terminal. We heard your words to the welcoming gang. Now you are going to tell *me* what you were so eager to tell elsewhere!"

If To'Frang was playing the Limiters' game deviously, then here was an excellent chance of reaching To'Kekrops' ears. But if the Commander was what he said, a leader of the opposition, then . . . Blake must walk a very perilous middle path *if* he could!

"The Limiters can not take me over. As you say, there were some important men of ours lost along the crosstime. If a big enough force from here could be tricked into hunting them—"

"On some inhospitable successor world?" To'Frang looked eager. "I do not think it will work. But, yes, I can see why it might be tried by men so lost. But your bait must be very good, Walker. To'Kekrops has no reason to go hunting for enemies he can dispose of merely by shutting down level-hopping. What kind of bait do you offer?"

"Erc Rogan!" Blake was forced into a corner from which the only exit was the truth. Though he would edit that truth to the best of his ability.

"Rogan? But Rogan is dead." To'Frang's tone was one of such confidence that had Blake not known the contrary he might have been convinced.

"And if he was not dead?"

"Yes." Again To'Frang stroked the surface of his desk, running his fingertips along the green line. "Yes, if Rogan were not dead, that would be bait to interest To'Kekrops, to make him send a force hunting. But Rogan *is* dead!"

"What proof of that have you?"

The long fingers were still. To'Frang glanced up, locked stares with Blake.

"There was a report tape. He was rayed. The man who lost his head and did it was erased two days ago."

"And the body?"

"There was no body." To'Frang's head jerked. An avid eagerness awoke in his face. "Rogan— Rogan escaped?"

"Let us think of one explanation for no body," Blake evaded. "If Rogan was almost through the hatch of a shuttle, if he was not killed, only wounded, if he made it to another level—"

"You know it—the truth!" To'Frang sprang to his feet again. For the first time the other three who had brought Blake to consciousness again crowded around, all of them intent upon what he might say. Were they eager because a failing cause might now produce a rallying point, or were they traitors avid to carry out the ultimate betrayal of the corps they had given allegiance to? At least Blake had their complete attention.

"I will tell you this much: Rogan *is* alive." Blake made a definite move in this blind game.

"Where?" To'Frang's hand hovered over the buttons on his desk as if he could summon the lost into this room by their prompt use.

"Safe—for now—on an uncoded level."

"Uncoded! But there is a code, there has to be! You have it?"

"With a whole world to search, what good would even having the code do?" Again Blake hedged. "Be assured that I can furnish To'Kekrops with a code and more—if I can see him personally."

"Rogan!" To'Frang breathed deeply as if he had been running. "You can get to To'Kekrops with that name, assuredly you can. And the great man himself can perhaps be sucked into a personal search. Yes, of course, yes! It is our best chance yet! Get to To'Kekrops. You *will* get to him with *that* story, Walker. Lessan!" The man who had slapped Blake moved forward another step. "Lessan, see what is going on out there, along the top floors."

The wardsman drew a wide white band from the front of his coverall, adjusted it about his right arm and slipped out into the corridor. To'Frang nodded to the others. One of them pulled seats drawer-fashion from the wall, and the other went to a dispenser and dialed meals, bringing out cover trays. In spite of the human disorganization in Headquarters, Blake saw, the machines which supplied the necessities of life were still in excellent working order. He ate heartily, the first real meal he could remember since the morning of the last day in Xomatl. And he had no idea when he would eat again. He had expected more questions from the Commander. But instead of any talk,

To'Frang appeared absorbed in the code buttons on his desk, running his fingers along their rows while sometimes his lips moved as if he worked problems in his head. One might judge that he was studying out some problem of crosstiming— and not by the regular methods.

Methodically Blake chewed and swallowed. If he dared believe that To'Frang was what he claimed to be, then perhaps he had found recruits to swell the ranks of Rogan's diehards. But if the Commander was merely To'Kekrops' tool, the sooner he was uncovered the better. One comment the other had made did not ring true: Blake did not believe that the Limiter leader could be lured away to level-hop himself. But that he would send a force to search for that member of the Hundred who was his most determined enemy and who would be the rallying head of any insurrection against his rebellion—yes. And that was what Blake's own plan counted on. But backed by adepts in mental control, To'Kekrops would believe that he needed only to dispatch a take-over force. The defeat of To'Kekrops would have to be here on Vroom, and Blake had yet to see how they could do it. This was a vast gamble on chance alone.

Of course, if he were lucky enough to get hand on a stunner, and a chance to remove the rebel leader, and an open way to a shuttle . . . But each of those wishes was more fantastic than the one preceding it.

The same guard who had dialed their meals collected the now empty trays and slid them down the disposal vent. As if that act was a signal, To'Frang looked up.

"Lessan's running late," he observed.

"We go up?" one of the hitherto silent guards suggested.

"Might be wise," the Commander assented. He went to the door, opened it cautiously and looked quickly both ways into the corridor. A jerk of his head was an order and Blake got to his feet, moving behind To'Frang and sandwiched between the two guards.

Most of the Headquarters offices were soundproof, but the halls were not. And hitherto, when he had walked along them, there had been the ebb and flow of noise, muffled voices, the sounds of machinery. Now there was only an intimidating silence. Most of the doors were firmly shut and To'Frang set a good pace. He did not turn to the anti-gravity lifts but sought the seldom-used, ladderlike emergency stairs behind concealing panel entrances.

They went up two floor levels, approaching the Commandant's office at the very top of Headquarters. Crowded together on a narrow landing, they waited for To'Frang to try the door. He pushed at it, but it gave only a little until one of the others lent his strength. They looked into a small room lined with shelves crowded with supply cartons of tapes and viewer film. But the obstruction that had barred the door lay on the floor.

His white-banded arm flung across his chest as if in a vain attempt to ward off death, Lessan sprawled there. He had been rayed, just like the tech Blake had found at the Project. The Commander stared down at the body; there was no mistaking his utter surprise. So deep was that amazement that Blake was convinced that his

own distrust was well-founded. The death of one
of his men, caught spying on the enemy, should
not have so completely astounded the Commander.

"Lessan!" The man at Blake's left pushed in,
went on one knee beside the body. "But why?"

"A tape-tap!" To'Frang half whispered. "He
had me tape-tapped!"

Blake was certain now concerning the other,
though he strove to conceal it. So the Commander
was one of the Limiter adherents! Perhaps he had
played such an undercover game for a long time.
But To'Kekrops, running true to form, trusted no
one. He had had his subordinate's office tape-
tapped, had heard or had reported to him all that
passed there. And something had made the new,
would-be ruler of Vroom ready to write To'Frang
off.

"They left him here," To'Frang continued to
stare at the body, "so we would know." The shock
of his find wore off a little and he glanced at Blake.
In that instant, the other knew all need for pretense was gone, that the Commander was done
with acting. And he knew, too, that the Commander believed that, in Blake, he had a chance to
redeem whatever mistake he had made.

"Take this one in!" He snapped the order.

The guard kneeling by Lessan merely glanced
up, and then down at the body again and
shrugged. His fellow was already backing to the
stair door. But in To'Frang's hand flashed a laser.

"You fools!" he spat at the guards. "They will
already have their orders to cut you down on
sight, you will have been 'vised throughout the
building. We go in there, where they will not

expect us, with this one in the lead. That way we have a chance. How can To'Kekrops think we are doublecrossing him if we do that? And he wants this one. He must have heard about Rogan from the tape, and this one will lead him right to Rogan."

The man on his knees looked at the one in the doorway and that one shrugged in resignation.

"They probably have us 'vised right enough," the latter said. "And if we deliver this Walker, who knows?"

"Deliver it is," his companion agreed.

To'Frang gestured them on with the hand that still held the rayer in full sight.

Thre was no escape for Blake with the three of them on guard. It would seem that he was about to reach his goal.

XVIII

To'Kekrops' features were familiar to anyone in Vroom, since they had appeared often on telecasts during the past year or so. But Blake had never seen the Limiter leader in person. And what he had expected was not quite in keeping with the man who sat stiff-backed at the end of the room that once had been dedicated to conferences between Committees of the Hundred and the Commandant of the Corps. All seats, save that now occupied by To'Kekrops, had been cleared away, leaving the center of the room open, an arrangement obviously intended to overawe those faced by the new fountainhead of law and authority.

Mind probe—far sharper and more intense than that which had greeted Blake at the terminal. But Blake had been prepared for that. To'Frang and the others halted, woodenstiff, as if the mental bolt had frozen them. But Blake walked on.

"They were right! You cannot be controlled." To'Kekrops regarded Blake, not as a man might survey an equal but as an explorer might center his attention on a new and outré form of life seen on another level.

"Turzor!"

A crackle of blue lightning cut through the air with the deadly threat, a death wall laid between them. This was no weapon of Vroom. But the man standing in the shadows by the wall plainly was adept in its use. Blake halted at that warning.

"I am told you have information for me,"

To'Kekrops came directly to the point, "that you told these fools you have the code of the level on which Rogan is hiding out, planning to use that as bait for me. How lackwitted do you think me, Blake Walker?"

There were two guards, the one with the flame weapon and another behind the Limiter leader; perhaps it was the second who was using the mind control. Blake had no weapon, no way of reaching the other by force, just by his wits. And at that moment he felt them singularly inept.

"If you had that via tape-tap, sir," he began, "then you heard only what I thought fit to tell those who brought me here. That is not the full truth."

To'Kekrops smiled. "So this is to be a discussion as to what is truth? I fear we have little time for philosophical subtleties, Walker."

"You want Rogan," Blake cut in baldly.

"That is true. I want Erc Rogan, preferably alive. He will provide excellent service to our cause. But—if necessary—dead. Rogan, yes, I want Rogan."

"Alive and level-hopping?"

"Alive he may be. Level-hopping? That is another question. At present we know his hideout. And if he takes to a shuttle again, well, that can be curtailed. We have already taken steps."

"And with a whole world to search while he builds up his own force in the meantime?" Blake felt overmatched; he had only To'Kekrops' hatred to play upon.

"A nuisance." The Limiter leader still smiled. "Just a nuisance, not much more. I have already admitted that, in my hands at this moment, he would have some small worth. But what is your offer? And the motive behind it?"

"If you know my name, you must know something of my past."

"That you are not of Vroom? Yes."

"That I was brought here against my will because your people could not plant false memories in me. That does not mean that I found the change altogether to my liking."

"So you harbor some resentment for those responsible? Possible—possible—"

To'Kekrops was playing with him, Blake knew. One step and the flamer would finish him as it had Lessan. Yet his inner warning held level; the Limiter Leader was not about to jump, not in the immediate future. That could only mean that he did want what Blake had to offer.

"There are rumors," Blake continued deliberately, "that once you have matters settled here, there will be a reorganization of the corps, a different method of dealing with successor worlds."

To'Kekrops' smile grew broader, was now a death's head grin.

"Rumors, rumors! We are never free of those! But do not let me interrupt you. What dazzling proposition have you to make now?"

"My own level has many opportunities for a man with backing. . . ."

"A disturbed world," To'Kekrops said, "makes for profits for those delving into its troubles, I agree. A man with backing might well rise to heights there. You build your argument on a firm base, Walker. But what of your part in the matter of Erc Rogan?"

"He is on an uncoded world—"

"To which I have the code now!"

"Have you time to search the whole world? I know where . . ."

"There are ways of learning that from you." The smile did not fade.

"I am blocked. A man can be forced to babble nonsense under pressure when he is broken. But the truth may not be in what he says."

"So once more we are back to that troublesome matter of truth. Well, what do you propose to do to facilitate matters concerning Rogan?"

"I will guide a party with a mind control. You can take him easily."

"Why you, Walker? You are not really needed."

"Because Rogan is blocked. Your control cannot take him, and the guard will not find him alive if they force it." Blake improvised feverishly. There was a slim chance of attracting To'Kekrops by such an offer to the point where the Limiter Leader might make a slip, just one slip!

"Why should Rogan trust you?"

"I brought out his daughters when your people marooned them. I volunteered to come here to contact those he thought might help him."

"Turzor!" The man with the flamer came into the center of the room. "Jargarli!" Now the one behind To'Kekrops' chair pushed forward.

"A suitable force, do you agree?" the Limiter leader asked.

Blake looked from one to the other. "Yes," he said flatly.

To'Kekrops nodded. "You are right. Jargarli can hold a dozen minds, perhaps more; he has not yet found his limit. And you have already witnessed Turzor's efficiency with a weapon imported crosstime. We have even more effective ones, of course, but as yet their production is so limited that we must depend upon these more primitive arms. You say you can deliver Rogan. Very well. Prove it!"

Blake shook his head. "No bargain is one sided. What is to prevent Turzor proving his markmanship on me when Rogan is delivered?"

"Nothing at all, of course. Save this—a thin string on which to hang your life! You have pointed out that you have certain possibilities on your former level—"

"A very thin thread, sir, one I do not trust at all."

This was it! Either Blake won some concession now or he lost the whole game. But to accept To'Kekrops' first proposition was immediate defeat.

"Very well. I shall give you your chance. Thus." He must have pressed the summoner button in the arm of his chair, for another guard entered the far door.

To'Kekrops spoke. "Give me one of those stunners."

The man vanished, returning in moments with a box containing a weapon like that Varlt had given Blake in Xomatl.

"One of our own newer inventions," the Limiter leader explained. "It has several unusual properties. One: it can be used only by the man who first takes it into his hand. Second: it shoots a ray that is a powerful narcotic, an improvement on the stunners of general issue. Also, it has one disadvantage which its inventor has not yet mastered: it cannot be reloaded, and it has only six shots. Take it up."

Blake did so, feeling again the sensation of the weapon adapting to him alone.

"Now you will turn, having paid attention to the fact that Turzor has you in the sights of his weapon, and you will fire five times at that wall. Fire!"

There was no choice but to obey. Blake pressed the button five times, the guard who had brought the stunner watching him closely. At the man's affirmative nod, To'Kekrops spoke again.

"Now you have your defense against Turzor, and nature has provided you with one against Jargarli. Are you satisfied?"

"As much as I can hope to be, sir."

"Sensible acceptance of matters as they are. Now, bring me Rogan and we shall talk again. Assuredly we shall!"

Blake's glimmer of a plan still depended too much on luck. However, it was now in motion. They came back to the terminal, to the shuttle that had brought Blake in. Under strict survey of the two guards, Blake set the code, checked it, punched the course keys. Their quarters were cramped; Jargarli had the twin seat, Turzor was behind Blake.

No one spoke as the cabin vibrated, became quiescent again. But Blake was thinking furiously, knowing that his companions could not read his mind. How well had Lo Sige set up the welcome party at the other end? And could it function againt Jargarli's mind control?

When the arrival light flashed on, he spoke to Turzor. "You had better be ready."

Jargarli sneered. "There are but three men out

there; already they are under my control. They will be awaiting my orders."

Turzor watched Blake, the flamer in his hands, ready, the wardsman could see, for any hostile move.

"You first," he ordered harshly.

Blake shook his head. "No, Jargarli first if he wishes, then you. With three men under control out there and only one shot left me, how do you expect me to start anything?"

Turzor did not seem disposed to accept that reasoning. But his fellow guard nodded. "They will move at him on my words. There is no chance for any attack on us."

Now, all depended on Blake's ability to move fast. Waste his single shot and he lost everything. He might have a better chance later, but he could not depend upon that.

The hatch opened; Jargarli dropped to the rock within the hollow sphere. Blake, with split-second timing, threw himself onto the cabin floor. Turzor half turned, took the force of the stun ray at throat level. He gave a choked cry; blue flame cut across the cabin wall, ceasing when his finger slipped from the weapon's firing button. Blake grabbed for the rayer.

Teborun came scrambling through the hatch, his face blank. Plainly he was under control. He made for Blake. Under such command there would be no stopping him as long as he was conscious. Blake twisted to one side as the other wardsman rushed him. He kicked out and Teborun stumbled, banging into the seat, the stiff clumsiness of a controlled man making him awkward in the cramped confines of the cabin.

Blake chopped out stiff-handed with one of the unarmed combat blows in which he had been so well trained. Teborun grunted, went down. Blake reversed the flamer and brought its butt down on the probe scout's head. One out of Jargarli's control.

But what if one of the two remaining controlled had a stunner? The odds were still in Jargarli's favor, and the Limiter could pick up and pull into the battle any other refugee with range of his mind. If they had not scattered as they planned— though surely Lo Sige must have taken care of that.

Blake turned to Turzor. The man was limp, almost impossible to handle but he would provide a shield. The wardsman tugged at the dead weight of the guard's body, propped him up with the support of his own shoulder behind him, and moved for the door.

As nearly as he could remember, the only cover out there was that of the parked shuttles—unless Jargarli could reach one of the passages leading out of the sphere. Although in that maze he would be lost unless he was able to summon a guide through the control.

Blake peered over Turzor's hunched shoulder. He heard the soft hiss of a dart, saw it sink into the stunned guardsman's flaccid arm. So, he faced at least one stunner. But he also sighted Jargarli moving backwards toward one of the other shuttles. Of course, to make sure of Blake, he would have to stay and direct his puppets in battle. And he could not do that if he removed himself from the scene.

Steadying the barrel of the flamer on Turzor's

shoulder, Blake fired. The sparkling blue lanced just inches over Jargarli's head, cutting into the surface of the machine he had thought to shelter in. The Limiter ducked and Blake fired a second time.

There was the smell of ozone and of overheated metal. Jargarli would not use that machine for cover. And the next was well to his left. A figure rushed from the right, heading for the hatch of the cabin and Blake. The wardsman shoved Turzor out, straight at the attacker. Together, they crashed on the rock.

"Stand!"

Blake enforced that order with another burst of fireworks, This so close to Jargarli that he cried out, perhaps seared by the edge of the beam.

"The next goes dead center," Blake called.

Jargarli was frozen in a half-crouch. He had lost his sneer; now he showed Blake the snarl of a cornered and vicious animal. But he was far from finished.

Blake went flat, that inner warning giving him the only defense he had. He heard the metallic ping of a dart striking somewhere within the cabin. Jargarli was still playing his controlled pawn.

Blake aimed another spear of blue flame, this time running along the rock of the floor. Jargarli stumbled back, unable to stand his ground against it. Right, left, right, Blake played him, forcing the Limiter into the wreckage of the other shuttle. And then what Blake had been gambling on happened. Jargarli's own peril cracked his hold over his pawn.

There was a startled cry to Blake's left. Jargarli's

head jerked in that direction. For a moment he was able to reassert control. Then he made one more jump away from the flamer, lost his balance and fell.

"Needle him!" Blake shouted. He wriggled over the edge of the hatch, got to his feet, and ran in a zigzag pattern lest some remnants of Jargarli's control still set the other at his throat. But the shot he feared did not come and he reached the fallen Limiter. Jargarli did not move. He might already be unconscious, but Blake made sure of that with the butt of the flamer.

"I don't know what you can do or if you can do it." Blake faced them: Erc Rogan; Marfy; Marva, who was pale and shrunken but more clear-eyed than he had ever seen her; Lo Sige; four of the other refugees, including Teborun who nursed an aching head. "But if you can, it is our key to Vroom and to To'Kekrops."

Rogan did not answer directly. Instead he glanced from his daughters to Lo Sige, to one or two of the others, as if awaiting their comments. It was Lo Sige who spoke first.

"We did what many claimed was impossible when we sent our call across levels. That was a uniting of power. Why could not such an effort be also a weapon? To'Kekrops is working through controllers, yes, and most of us are susceptible to control attack. But it works both ways; they can be influenced, too."

"You used the call because Marfy, Marva, and I were linked." Rogan appeared to be thinking aloud. "So you had a definite focus at which to aim."

"We shall have focuses aplenty in Vroom once we get there, and probe waves to ride back to their sources. Now we have a specimen here to practice on."

Blake could not follow their entwined thought as they consulted without words. Nor was he one of the team they finally put together after much testing. In the end, their weapon was a strange one. Lo Sige formed the center of that odd attack, Marfy and Marva his immediate backing; Rogan was one wing; and the other was another wardsman, a fantastically clad merchant from a world Blake had never heard of. Only these five could mesh and hold the strangest offense and defense that crosstime must ever have seen.

Two of the control boards of the shuttles, one of them the partially wrecked one, were cannibalized to create the thing of wires and plates Blake wore, outside that "weapon" but still part of any battle to come to defend the others with the flamer and his own immunity to control. Once they disembarked in Vroom, they hoped they would be able to short-circuit the adepts To'Kekrops used to command his prisoners.

Teborun and another scout took a fourth machine, with orders to range time and pick up as many of the marooned as they could—Rogan had listed those who had special talents he needed—and ferry them into Vroom terminal.

They had used their device on Jargarli and proved that it worked with him. Now they were ready to go.

It was a tight squeeze in the cabin of the shuttle, but this was the machine expected in Vroom and they dared take no other. As they went into a spin, all eyes but Blake's closed. He could feel the force building up around him. His head ached, he experienced the sensation of being whirled around and around in the rapids of a raging river. Yet even under this pressure he did not crack.

"Terminal," he said aloud, breaking into the trance of his companions.

"Now!" Had Blake heard that with his ears or his mind? He was not sure, but it was like a shout within him. Holding the flamer to his side in half concealment, he unfastened the hatch and jumped out.

There was a reception committee right enough. But just a little too eager. Blake had taken precautions. Needlers hissed, but Blake had already dropped to his hands and knees. He need fear assault only for those first fleeting seconds.

The men who had been waiting there, ample proof of To'Kekrops' treachery, reeled back from the shuttle as a wave of blast force was emitted from the machine. Weapons dropped as several put their hands to their heads, rolled on the ground. Blake darted forward, grabbed at the stunners, began to aim and fire, using darts even on those crying out as they lay.

"Ready," he called into the cabin.

They came out, walking as if still tranced, passing unheeding the now unconscious men. Blake realized that his task was doubled. So sunk were the five in the concentration of holding and aiming their countercontrol, that the physical defense of the party must rest with him alone.

Three men burst out of a doorway. One shouted as he sighted the bodies on the ground. Blake fired. Two of the attackers staggered out into the terminal and went down to join the earlier victims. The third jumped back within the doorway. He might escape to give the alarm.

But the spear, five minds united in one purpose, marched on. Blake attempted both to scout and protect the rear. That, he decided, was impossible. He shot twice at men in the hall ahead, bringing one down. Then they had free passage to the gravity lift. Lo Sige dialed a destination signal. They rose at the nerve-shattering speed of emergency, shooting up past all the floors and corridors to the crown of Headquarters.

"He is there, waiting," Rogan said. "He thinks of escape . . ."

"He cannot. Do not let him!" Marfy cried. Her eyes were again closed; she held to her sister with one hand, and the other, moving out blindly, grasped Blake's sleeve, anchoring him to her with tense force.

For a long moment they stood so. Blake was convinced that their will, one formed of many, was holding To'Kekrops to await their coming.

The lift came to a halt, its door grated open.

"No!" Blake interposed his body between the gate and Lo Sige's advance. "No!"

He was just in time. A pattern of violence, which could only have been woven by another flamer, made a net of vicious light, but it had not caught them. These rays flew upward. Weapons, still spitting fire, moved through the air. They homed on the invaders, rose again, now pointing away, still firing, but moving ahead in some mindless life of their own, seeking now those who had earlier owned them. There were screams of terror such as Blake had never heard before. But

his own warning had subsided; their path was
clear.

Once before he had seen a battle of hallucination combined with the force of esper powers, that
one between Lo Sige and the outlaw he had
hunted across many worlds. But this was far
worse. The corridor before them wavered. They
might well have been marching through one successor world after another, in vivid, fantastic, and
horrible sequence. Blake reeled, staggered. But
Marfy still held his arm. And he sensed that the
nightmares that were visible to him were not the
same for her. Yet he dared not close his eyes to any
of them lest they vanish and the real enemy be
revealed weapon in hand, waiting.

He did not remember entering the council
chamber. He was not even sure he was there, for
the walls changed size and shape and the room
filled and emptied with forms and figures he saw
only dimly, knowing only a fierce desire not to see
them clearly.

Afterward Blake could never give a successful
account of that struggle. He was on the fringe of a
convulsion that distorted nature, form, and substance as he knew it. The alien quality of the void
in which that engagement was fought blinded
him to the warfare. It was doubtful if any mortal
could have witnessed that struggle with open
eyes.

When he could see clearly once again there was
the solid feel of floor under him and walls were no
longer eddying as if they were wind-tossed
smoke. Blake crouched, his hands empty of the
flamer—for what weapon of metal, man-made,
was useful in a battle of hallucination?

There was the chair in which To'Kekrops had sat. And in it still lolled a limp thing which pawed at itself and gave forth a thin, wailing mewl, a sound echoed by other things which crept aimlessly about on all fours or sprawled, their hands feebly beating the air.

But in the center of this room that the Limiters' leader had stripped to lend majesty to his own cause still stood those five. Now they shivered, clung to one another, displaying the faces of those who wake from bitter, heartpounding nightmares.

"It—it is done." Rogan's lips moved, but the dead tone that issued from between them was not his usual voice.

Blake gazed at the enemy, not sure just what had happened to To'Kekrops and those he had summoned to back him in the final defense. It was done if this was the last of the enemy. Done! But what had they done here, striving as they had striven? He had not been a part of the spear, but his idea had helped to forge it, his the instigation of its use. What had they done—or loosed?

"What do we do now?" Had he asked that aloud in his bewilderment or thought it? Minds . . . thoughts . . . fearful things . . . weapons . . .

"Do?" Lo Sige turned his head. A measure of sense and reason was back in the senior wardsman's eyes. It was as if he had dragged himself free of quicksand, was thankful he had won safety, yet did not quite yet believe in that safety. "Do?" he repeated. "Why, now we pick up the pieces."

"Pieces?" echoed Rogan. His arms were about his daughters' shoulders; he drew them closer to him. "Pick up the pieces, yes, and there are many of them."

Blake rose. For a moment some trick of memory brought back the alien otherness that had captured this hall for a space. But the recall was gone in a flash. Yes, there were pieces, and some of them might still exist in shapes which spelled trouble. He looked around for the flamer. It was going to be a long day or night—or whatever hour had struck now—for Vroom.

Andre Norton

☐ 12314	Crossroads Of Time	$1.95
☐ 16664	Dragon Magic	1.95
☐ 33704	High Sorcery	1.95
☐ 37291	Iron Cage	1.95
☐ 45001	Knave Of Dreams	1.95
☐ 47441	Lavender Green Magic	1.95
☐ 67556	Postmarked The Stars	1.25
☐ 71100	Red Hart Magic	1.95
☐ 78015	Star Born	1.75

Available wherever paperbacks are sold or use this coupon.

WITCH WORLD SERIES

89705	**Witch World**	$1.95
87875	**Web of the Witch World**	$1.95
80805	**Three Against the Witch World**	$1.95
87323	**Warlock of the Witch World**	$1.95
77555	**Sorceress of the Witch World**	$1.95
94254	**Year of the Unicorn**	$1.95
82356	**Trey of Swords**	$1.95
95490	**Zarsthor's Bane** (Illustrated)	$1.95